# It was too good to be true.

Devon ran her hand ever so lightly over the bassinet.

"This is wonderful," she said in a small, halting voice, afraid to speak up because she thought her voice would crack. "Where did you get all this?"

"Miss Joan is very resourceful," Cody told her matter-of-factly. "Technically," he specified, "these are all on loan—except for the diapers, of course."

"I don't care if they're on loan," Devon told him. "The fact that I can use them even for a little while is just wonderful," she added, tearing up completely.

Nothing made Cody feel more helpless than tears. "Oh, hey, you're not going to cry, are you?"

"No," she said, and then promptly had several fat tears go cascading down both of her cheeks.

At a loss, not knowing what else to do, Cody took her into his arms and just held her, saying nothing. He just wanted her to know that he was there for her, no matter what she needed.

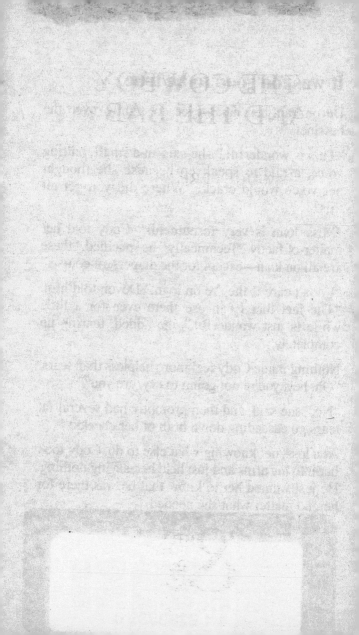

# THE COWBOY AND THE BABY

BY
MARIE FERRARELLA

First Published in Great Britain 2016
By Mills & Boon, an imprint of HarperCollins*Publishers*
1 London Bridge Street, London, SE1 9GF

© 2016 Marie Rydzynski-Ferrarella

ISBN: 978-0-263-92029-1

23-1016

Our policy is to use papers that are natural, renewable and recyclable products and made from wood grown in sustainable forests. The logging and manufacturing processes conform to the legal environmental regulations of the country of origin.

Printed and bound in Spain
by CPI, Barcelona

**Marie Ferrarella** is a *USA TODAY* bestselling and RITA®
Award-winning author who has written more than two
hundred and fifty books for Mills & Boon, some under the
name Marie Nicole. Her romances are beloved by fans
worldwide. Visit her website, www.marieferrarella.com.

To
Dr. Steve Kang
For Giving Me Hope
That I Could
Wear High Heels Again

# *Prologue*

Cody McCullough didn't like being late.

Ever.

It was a work ethic his big brother Connor had instilled in all of them. Connor had insisted on it that first time he had gathered them all together to tell them that, despite the recent death of their father, they were still going to be a family, still go on living under one roof. Connor had just turned eighteen at the time. That ultimately meant that, as the oldest, Connor was willing to give up his dreams of going away to college in order to become their guardian.

There was no one else to turn to and, besides, Connor had never been one to believe in buck-passing.

Taking care of three younger siblings and a modest cattle ranch was a hell of a responsibility to take on for an eighteen-year-old, so the rest of them—Cody, Cole and Cassidy—figured that the least they could do was not give Connor a hard time about anything, including the rules he saw fit to set down and enforce.

Connor's Code, they had all come to agree, was there for their own good. If they were to survive in a world that could—all too easily—be rough and cruel, they had to pull together.

And in exchange for not giving Connor any grief, their older brother returned the favor. He backed them whenever he could and never made them feel as if they were victims of a cold fate. He taught them that they were the masters of their own destinies. They just had to fight a little harder to forge them.

Even so, when Cody had decided to do something different with his life—change his career path to become a deputy—he was certain that Connor would voice his objections, or at least display a degree of displeasure with his choice.

Instead, Connor had heard him out when he made his case. At the end, he had nodded, saying, "If that's what you want to do, do it. You change your mind, the ranch is always going to be here for you. But if you're going to be a deputy, I want you to be the best damn deputy you can be. I don't want to hear anyone telling me that the sheriff regrets the day he took you on as Alma's replacement."

And Cody had promised to give the job nothing less than his best—which had turned out to be a challenge.

Alma Rodriguez Tyler might have been a small woman, as well as the first female deputy that Forever, Texas, had ever had, but Cody would have been the first one to say that she had left some pretty big boots to fill.

Even so, he had taken to the job like the proverbial duck to water. Cody discovered that he really loved it. Loved putting on the uniform, the badge. Loved being a deputy the way he hadn't ever really loved being a rancher.

The only part of ranching that *was* near and dear

to his heart was the horses. He loved riding, loved becoming one with the animal beneath him. While his other siblings gradually shifted over to getting around in the family truck or the second-hand Jeep they had all chipped in to buy, Cody loved riding. He had ever since he'd been a toddler and his late father, Josh, had picked him up and put him on the back of his first horse, a sleepy-eyed old mare named Libby.

Still, like any young man of twenty-five, Cody had given in to conformity and saved up to buy his own Jeep in the interest of the image he knew he had to project as one of Sheriff Rick Santiago's deputies.

Not that there was all that much for the sheriff's department to do. It wasn't as if Forever, population of a little over five hundred people these days, was exactly a hotbed of either criminal activity or underhanded dealings. There was the occasional argument that escalated to trading blows, and of course there was Miss Elizabeth, an eighty-nine-year-old widow who, from time to time, would be found wandering the streets of Forever, sleepwalking in her nightgown.

For the most part, theirs was a quiet little town. He and the two deputies, Joe Lone Wolf and Gabe Rodriguez, were seen more as friends than as lawmen.

But a man's word was his bond and Cody believed in being at his desk at the beginning of each workday because he was supposed to, not because he was waiting for some minor crime wave to break out so he could jump into action.

As fate would have it, his spirit might have been more than willing to arrive on time, but his Jeep's was not. For some reason, the vehicle had simply refused to turn over when he put his key in the ignition, despite the fact that the town's sole mechanic—thought to be a veritable wizard when it came to machinery—had overhauled it and pronounced it good as new.

Cody knew everything there was to know about horses and absolutely nothing when it came to car engines. After one more futile attempt to rouse the engine, he'd pocketed his key and thrown a saddle on Flint, a golden palomino he had raised from a colt.

A couple of minutes later, he was headed toward Forever at a quick gallop.

Entirely focused on not being late, Cody had almost missed seeing the beat-up pickup truck. The truck, which had definitely seen better days, was pulled over to the far side of the road. And even if he had seen it, it was in such poor condition, he would have just assumed it was abandoned.

Cody had already ridden past it when he thought he heard a scream.

Pulling up Flint's reins, he paused, cocked his head and listened again.

Nothing.

He was just about to chalk it up to either his imagination or the summer wind, which could, at times, make a mournful sound. Cody was on the verge of lightly kicking the palomino's flanks and resuming his journey when he heard it again.

This time there was no doubt in his mind. What he'd heard was definitely a scream. It was loud, full-bodied and strong enough to not just make his blond hair stand on end, but to send a hard shiver down his spine, as well.

Automatically putting his hand over his holster to assure himself that he had remembered to strap on his weapon before heading out, Cody turned his horse around and galloped right back toward the clearly *not* abandoned pickup truck. Excitement coursed through his body.

Someone was in trouble.

# Chapter One

Oh God, this was such a bad idea. She shouldn't have driven out looking for him in her condition.

"Yeah, like you really had a choice," Devon Bennett mocked herself, sarcasm saturating each word.

Independent to a fault, accustomed to handling everything that came her way, Devon could never have resisted looking for Jack when she woke up to find him gone from the motel room.

At first, she'd thought he'd just gone out to get them breakfast—but he wouldn't have needed to take their suitcase for that. And it was missing, along with her credit cards and all the money out of her purse.

He did leave her the truck. But that wasn't because he'd had an attack of conscience, or even because she was carrying his baby and was due to deliver in about a week or so. Being coldly honest with herself, Devon knew that Jack hadn't taken the truck for one reason and one reason only. The truck was still there, parked right outside of the rundown motel, because Jack couldn't find the keys to it.

He wasn't able to find them because she'd had this uneasy feeling that Jack was having second thoughts about the plans they had laid out for their future.

Not knowing what Jack might impulsively decide to do, she had tucked the keys to the truck under her pillow—smack in the center so that even if he did suspect they were there, he would have had to move her in such a way that she was certain to wake up.

Looking back now as she scanned the desolate area—weren't there supposed to be some *people* around this forsaken wilderness?—Devon couldn't have said exactly what had possessed her to hide the keys, but maybe, somewhere deep down, she didn't really trust Jack anymore. Oh, he'd smiled a lot and talked about these grand plans he had for the two of them, promising that everything would be wonderful once they got to Houston.

They'd left Taos, New Mexico, because Jack had come into their small apartment one morning telling her that he'd lined up another job—a much better job—and it was waiting for him in Houston. They'd been together for almost three years and they'd gotten engaged after four pregnancy tests had yielded the same answer: positive.

At the time, she'd thought that finding out she was pregnant would send Jack packing, but Jack surprised her. He stayed.

He'd even looked as if he was happy about it. The baby, the engagement, the promise of a new job—he made it sound as if all they needed was a new beginning to make everything work out.

She'd had no reason to doubt him.

No reason except perhaps the nagging, sinking feeling in the pit of her stomach—something apart from morning sickness for a change—warning her that maybe, just maybe it was too good to be true.

And she had learned a long time ago that if something seemed too good to be true, then it usually wasn't.

"*Usually?* Always. It's always too good to be true," Devon retorted, the realization all but tearing her up.

Tears began to gather in her eyes, threatening to fall, to make her come apart. Devon struggled to hold herself together. She didn't even know where she was going, other than just heading somewhere "due east" because that was the direction they'd been driving in when they'd pulled up to that sad little motel.

It hadn't been her first choice. She had located an actually decent hotel that was about ten miles up the road, but Jack had vetoed it, saying that hotel would eat into "their" capital.

The only capital Jack was acquainted with was the first letter to his name. The money was hers— or it had been before he'd taken it, along with the gold cross her mother, Amy, had left her and the earrings that might or might not have been worth something. Whatever actual dollar amount the jewelry was worth, both pieces had meant the world to her because they were all she had left from her mother.

But to Jack the jewelry was just something to be converted into cash at his first opportunity.

So he'd left her with her truck and taken everything else. Because she'd had no money to pay the desk clerk, she'd been forced to sneak out while dawn was still creeping in. She'd assuaged her conscience by promising herself that she'd find him, that no good, sweet-talking thief—not because she wanted him back, but because she wanted to pay the motel clerk and, more than that, recover her mother's cross and earrings.

But where the hell could he have gotten to?

And where on earth was she?

When she'd tried to pinpoint her location on her smartphone's GPS, Devon could have sworn that if her phone had had actual hands, it would have been scratching its head.

She was in the middle of nowhere—and getting more deeply entrenched.

More tears stung her eyes.

"Serves me right for thinking that just once in my life, things were going to go WELLL! OMIGOD!"

The pain, sudden and sharp and completely unexpected, had come leaping out at her from nowhere.

Devon had been upset and overwrought and paying attention to the road, not to the signals her body was sending her. In her defense, she'd been experiencing strange sensations and odd little pains off and on for a while now.

Scanning her memory bank now, she realized that her lower half had been feeling very, very strange, but then, that could have easily described the way her bottom had been feeling ever since she'd found that she was pregnant.

Focused on hunting Jack down, she'd had no reason to believe that this "strange" feeling was any different than all the other strange feelings she'd been experiencing all along.

Except that it *was* different.

She'd never quite had this pain before. Never felt like two giant hands had each taken hold of one of her legs and were now about to make a wish just before they pulled them apart in two opposite directions.

"Can't you wait, Michael?" she begged, addressing her very swollen abdomen by the name she had selected. Not that she knew the baby's gender. She'd just assumed that it was male because it had been giving her such a hard time from the moment she'd conceived him. "You're not supposed to be here yet and, in case you haven't noticed, we're in the middle of nowhere. I can't do this alone. Sorry to disappoint you, little boy, but I am *not* the pioneer type.

"There, you have had the worst of it," she told her unborn son as the pain settled down a little. "Except that your father's a rat, but we'll talk about that later. Like in a week and a half," she stressed. "*Please* wait a week and a half."

She went on reasoning with the baby that seemed intent on kicking its way out now. "Please, please, PLEEEASE!" she shrieked, unable to contain the pain.

Sweat was pouring down from her brow and her tears were mingling with it, pooling along the hollow of her throat.

Devon couldn't believe that this was actually happening, that she was going to die in the middle of nowhere, giving birth.

"This is *not* happening now," she yelled at her stomach. "Do you hear me? I'm your mother and I forbid you to come out!"

Another scream tore from her lips, taking a tremendous toll on her body. She was beginning to feel as if she was hallucinating.

"You're not going to listen, are you?" she asked

weakly. A deep, frustrated sigh emerged from the center of her very core. "Not even born and you're already a typical male."

The next wave of pain completely stole her breath away, making her pant.

Making her panic.

"No, no panicking. Panicking is bad," she admonished herself, trying desperately to exercise some measure of control, putting mind over matter.

But it wasn't helping.

Nothing was helping. She was coming apart at the seams, literally, and nobody would ever know what had happened to her.

The word throbbed in her brain.

*Nobody.*

The few friends she had all thought that she'd run off with Jack to Texas. They'd never know that she died before she got to her destination.

And she had no family. An only child, she'd lost her father when she was seven and her mother when she was a senior in high school.

So there was no one to worry about her.

No one cared.

That was probably why she'd been such an easy target for Jack. She'd always thought of herself as an independent soul, but the truth of it was she was lonely. She'd wanted to matter to someone, just *one* someone. And Jack had pretended that she mattered to him.

Tall, dark and handsome with an easy grin, Jack had drifted into her life and then taken her along for the ride.

She'd been a total fool, Devon thought disparagingly.

Perspiration was beginning to soak through her clothing. She didn't know if the sun was hot, or if only she was. The end result was the same. Her clothes were damp.

"I thought your daddy loved me. Turns out he loved my meager little savings account. But we'll find him, you and I. We'll catch up to him and force him to give back all that money because you're going to need diapers—and food.

"Who am I kidding?" she said despondently. "We're not getting out of here alive. I'm sorry, Michael. Sorry to have done this to you. Sorry to have saddled you with a daddy who's a deadbeat. SORRYYYY!"

The pain was so bad that she'd almost bitten right through her bottom lip this time around.

She was clutching and clawing at anything she could find within reach. The pain was growing stronger, threatening to swallow her up completely. As it was, she was on the verge of passing out.

This was more than she could endure.

This was—

"Ma'am?"

Devon screamed again, this time in fear. A moment ago, there'd been no one here, not even a prairie dog. Now someone—or more accurately, some*thing*— was leaning in through her rolled-down truck window, peering in and apparently talking to her.

"Oh God, now I'm seeing things," she cried, doing her best to disappear into the cracked seat cushion. "Talking horses. Maybe I've already died."

Belatedly, Cody realized that the woman in the cab of the truck was looking at Flint. She sounded as if she was delirious.

Dismounting, he tied the horse's reins to the back of the vehicle and returned to the open window. He looked in.

The woman was drenched and looked almost wild-eyed. "Are you alone?" Cody asked her.

"Not a horse, an angel," Devon realized out loud. The next moment, she closed her eyes tight as she felt yet another huge contraction coming. This one had all the signs of being even bigger than the last. "A hunky angel," she said to herself. "This is Texas, what did I EXPECCTTT?"

For a second, Cody could only stare at her in complete awe. Even wracked with pain, the dark-haired woman was beautiful. But he'd never seen a woman *this* pregnant before. She looked as if she was just about to pop at any moment.

"No disrespect, lady," he began politely, really wishing someone else was with him right now— Cassidy, for instance.

Women related to each other at a time like this. Or maybe Connor. Nothing rattled Connor. He could handle anything. Still, wishing didn't change anything. Cody was the only other human being out here and he was going to handle this.

He put a sympathetic expression on his face. "But what are you doing out here by yourself in your condition?"

She had no idea what possessed her. She didn't even remember doing it, but, suddenly, Devon found herself grabbing the front of the inquisitive angel's shirt and yanking on it with all the strength she had. She yanked on it so hard that she almost dragged him right in through the window.

"DYING!" she yelled back.

"So you *are* having contractions?" the cowboy asked.

*Great, a Rhodes scholar.* "What…gave it…away?" she panted, desperately trying to get away from the pain or at least ahead of it. She failed. It insisted on following her.

Cody ignored the woman's sarcastic comeback. "How far apart are your contractions?" he asked.

Devon was arching in her seat. No one had ever said it was going to hurt this badly. "Not…far… ENOUGH!"

Cody looked out into the horizon, in the direction he'd been riding when he'd heard her screams. Forever was about five, maybe seven, miles away.

"There's a clinic in town," he told her. "I can get you there fast."

But all she could do was shake her head—violently— from side to side. He'd never get her there in time. Besides, the idea of movement made everything worse.

"No…time," she panted. "Baby…coming… NOOOWWWW!"

That was what he was afraid of.

Mentally, Cody rolled up his sleeves. Connor always insisted that they face all their challenges head-on, not hide behind excuses or shirk their responsibilities. This woman obviously needed him.

Whether he liked it or not, it was just as simple as that. He took a deep, fortifying breath.

"Okay, then," Cody told her. "Let's do this."

Maybe he *was* better than an angel, Devon thought. "You're…a…doctor?" she asked, digging her nails in the cab's seat again, bracing herself for what she now knew was coming.

"No," Cody answered honestly, "but I helped birth a few calves on the ranch before I became a sheriff's deputy."

Terrific, he was a cowboy. Just her luck. "I'm… having…a…BABYYY," she cried, arching again, "not…a…CAAALF!"

Cody did his best to give her a confident smile. "Same difference," he assured her.

No, it wasn't, she thought. Not by a long shot. "I… am…in…so…much…TROUBLE!" Devon screamed, all but biting a hole in her lip.

"I know this is scary," he told her.

"You…don't…know…the…HALF…OF…IT!" she retorted, trying her best not to give way to hysteria as she dug her nails into his forearm.

He did what he could to comfort her. "I think I can guess," he told her, then began to introduce himself. "My name is Cody, and I'll be delivering your baby today," he ended with a warm smile.

At this point, Devon was no longer worrying about whether or not she was hallucinating. If this hallucination could help her get rid of this incredible piercing pain she was experiencing through her lower half, then she was all for it.

"PLEEEEASE!" she all but begged.

"What's your name?" Cody asked as he carefully climbed into the truck's cab, coming in from the passenger side. He gently shifted her so that she wasn't behind the steering wheel anymore.

What difference did her name make? "Are…you… filling…out…a…form?" Devon cried in disbelief.

"Just thought it'd be easier for both of us if I knew your name before I got personal," he replied.

She'd thought that she was way past embarrassment. This was another low. Devon closed her eyes. "Oh…Lord…"

But the pain ramped up, becoming so intense that she was quickly at the point where she would do anything to get beyond it. "DEVON! MY NAME'S DEVON!"

"Nice to meet you, Devon." He braced himself for what he was about to say and do. "I'm going to have to have to lift up your skirt."

She knew that. He didn't have to narrate his actions, she thought in mounting agitation. She just wanted this to be over. If this baby wasn't coming out soon, Devon was certain that she was going to die out here in the middle of nowhere.

"Say…that…to…all…the…girls?" she managed to get out without screaming at him.

"Just the pregnant ones I find in abandoned trucks on the side of the road," he said dryly.

Feeling somewhat awkward about it, Cody slipped the woman's underwear off, all the while telling himself that this was nothing personal, that he had to do it in order to help her bring this baby into the world.

As he drew the material off her legs, he glanced at the hand that was clutching at him. It was the woman's left hand and he saw that there was a ring on it. Not a wedding ring, but a rather tiny engagement ring. At least, he assumed that's what it was. The stone at the center was missing.

He couldn't help wondering if the baby's father was just temporarily missing from this scene—or if there was more to the story than that.

It was a story that was going to have to wait for another day, Cody told himself. From what he saw, Devon appeared to be completely dilated and ready to become a mother.

"You're going to have to bear down and start pushing now," he told her.

She didn't answer him. And then he realized why. As he saw the perspiration popping out all along her brow, she ground out a bloodcurdling noise.

Cody saw that she was already complying with his instructions.

# Chapter Two

Devon's face had turned a bright shade of red. In Cody's estimation, she was pushing too hard and too long. She had to take a break. Otherwise he had a feeling that she was going to rupture something.

"Okay, now rest," he told her. She didn't seem to hear him. Her eyes were screwed shut and her face was growing even redder. "Stop pushing!" Cody ordered more loudly.

Worn-out, Devon fell back against the seat, her hair damp and plastered against her brow. She was panting really hard.

"You...tell...the...cow...that...too?" she gasped.

Devon couldn't remember *ever* feeling this exhausted. She'd pushed so hard, she was seeing spots dancing before her eyes.

"No. I saw this on a medical drama on TV," he confessed. It was the summer he'd broken his leg and was laid up with nothing else to do. He'd picked up a lot of miscellaneous information that came in handy at the oddest times. Like now.

"Better...and...better," Devon retorted. This would have been funny if she wasn't so scared and in so much pain.

The next second, she went rigid again as another scream pierced the air. Without waiting for him to say anything, she began to bear down again.

Cody knew better than to interfere unless it was absolutely necessary, so he counted the seconds off out loud.

When she'd gone past the limit, he ordered, "Stop!"

This creature inside her—she'd ceased thinking of it as a baby—had taken charge of her body and she couldn't control the urge to push it out.

"I...CAN'T!"

"Breathe through your mouth." When she didn't seem to hear him, Cody put his hands on either side of her face and made her look at him. "Listen to me, unless you want to start possibly hemorrhaging, *breathe through your mouth*!" he ordered. "Like this."

And he proceeded to show her, recalling what he'd seen on that program he'd watched during his summer of forced confinement.

He could only pray he got it right.

Cody saw anger in the woman's eyes. Anger mingled with fear, but then she began to do what he'd told her. Blowing air out of her mouth, she stopped pushing for a moment.

And then he felt her growing rigid again. Her whole body looked as if it was in the throes of another contraction.

"Another one?" he asked.

It was a rhetorical question, but she answered anyway. "YES!" she hissed as she dug deep into her core to find the energy to expel this child out of her body once and for all.

"I see the head!" Cody declared in wonder as he tried his best to encourage her.

"Isn't...there...any...more?" she cried sharply.

She was going to die like this, she was certain of it. She could feel herself growing weaker and weaker as she seemed to float in and out of her head.

"There's more," he assured her. "There's more!" This time he said it because she was pushing again. Pushing and screaming. "You're almost there," he encouraged.

"AAAARRRGGGHHH!"

The word shattered the atmosphere as it accompanied the emergence of the infant who was sliding out of her body.

Euphoric, exhausted and close to delirious, Devon panted hard, trying to regain her breath. Trying to hear something beyond the sound of her heart, which was pounding like mad.

"He's not...crying," Devon said, panicking. "Why isn't...my...baby...crying?"

Cody didn't answer her. He was too busy trying to get the tiny human being he was holding in his arms to do just that.

Turning the infant over so that it was facing the ground, Cody patted the baby's back, then turned it over again to check its airway.

Quickly clearing it with his forefinger, he held the baby in one arm while unbuttoning his shirt with the other.

Devon attempted to use her elbows to prop herself up so she could see what was going on. She didn't have enough strength left to manage it.

"What—what are you doing?" Devon demanded

weakly. Why was this man getting undressed? Fresh fear vibrated through her.

Parting the tan deputy shirt, Cody pressed the baby against his bare skin, all the while still massaging the tiny back.

A tiny whimper just barely creased the air. And then there was a cry. An indignant, lusty cry, followed by another one.

Cody breathed a sigh of relief. His own heart was racing in triumph and elation.

"She's going to be all right!" he declared.

Confusion slipped over Devon's face. "She?" Devon questioned, unable to process the deputy's words for a moment.

Shrugging out of his shirt one sleeve at a time, he passed the infant from one arm to the other as he did it. Once he had the shirt off, he wrapped the material around the newborn.

"Your baby's a girl," he told Devon. She was also the first infant he'd delivered and he was filled with a warm glow he couldn't begin to describe.

"Michael's a girl?" Devon asked, confused and happy at the same time. It was over. The baby was out and it was over! She realized that she was crying again.

"You might want to think about changing that name," Cody advised. Looking down at the infant, he smiled. "This is your mama," he told the baby as he transferred her into Devon's arms.

Her head spinning, feeling like someone in a dream, Devon carefully accepted the swaddled infant into her arms. She felt completely drained as she held the infant against her.

She did her best to smile at her daughter. "Hi, baby."

Out of the corner of her eye, Devon thought she saw the man who had come to her rescue pull a knife out of the sheath within his boot. A wave of new fear shimmied through her.

"What are you going to do?" she asked in a horrified whisper, unable to gather the strength for anything louder.

Having struck a match—he always kept a book of matches in his pocket, although he rarely used them—Cody was passing the blade of his knife back and forth over the flame.

"The umbilical cord is still attached," he told her with an easy smile. "I figure it might get in the way after a bit."

Even though it was hard for her to focus, Devon was watching his every move. Her arms weakly tightened around the baby. "Will it hurt?"

"Can't really say for sure," Cody told her honestly, "but I don't think so." He looked up at her. "Got any alcohol in the glove compartment?"

Was he looking to toast the successful birth? Now? Had she not felt so exhausted, she might have seriously considered trying to get out of the truck with her baby.

"No," she cried.

"Too bad." He carefully lifted the umbilical cord at the baby's end. "It might have been good to disinfect the area, but this should be okay for now."

And then, just like that, before she could ask Cody when he was going to do it—he'd separated the infant from the cord. She felt the remainder, no longer of any use, being expelled out of her own body.

Sweating profusely, Devon didn't realize that she had taken in a sharp breath until she released it.

"That's it?" she asked.

Cody nodded. "As far as I know."

The reality of the situation and what he had just miraculously been a part of finally hit him. It took Cody a moment to get his breath back. The tiny infant nestled in the crook of Devon's arm looked at peace, as if she had always been a part of the scene rather than just newly arrived.

"How are you feeling?" Cody asked Devon, concerned. The color seemed to be draining out of her.

"Woozy," she answered. "Wonderful, but really, really light-headed."

"Well, you did good," he told her. Very carefully, he reached out and, ever so lightly, stroked the baby's downy head. "Feels like peach fuzz," he commented quietly with a warm smile.

"It'll grow," Devon told him, struggling not to slur. "My mom said… I was bald until I…was one, now it grows like…crazy."

She sounded exhausted. He didn't blame her. He was feeling a little depleted himself. He just had one more question for her. "What are you going to call her?" he asked.

She barely heard him at first, and then his words replayed themselves in his head.

"I don't know," Devon answered honestly. "I was… really sure I was having…a boy, so all I have…are… boys' names."

A thought hit him. It seemed almost like fate,

he thought. "My mom's name was Layla. I always thought that was a pretty name."

"Layla," Devon repeated weakly. "You're…right… It…is…pretty." She looked down at the baby in her arms. Her daughter was looking up at her with wide, wide blue eyes. A peacefulness was descending over Devon. Her mind began to drift, but she did her best to focus. "Layla," she repeated again to see if the name fit. It seemed to.

"You like that?" The infant made a tiny noise. It wasn't in response, but Devon took it that way. She glanced up at the man who had been there for her when he could have just kept going. "Looks…like it's…unanimous."

"What were you doing out here by yourself?" he asked. If he'd been in her place, he wouldn't have been driving around in the middle of nowhere. Where was the man who belonged to that ring? To that baby?

"Looking…for a cowboy…to deliver…my baby," she told him weakly.

She wasn't going to tell him, he thought. Well, that was her business, he supposed. He could respect that. Cody was just glad that he had been running late this morning. If his Jeep hadn't decided to die, who knew what might have happened to the pregnant woman?

He glanced at her face. She appeared frighteningly pale. "You need to be checked out by a doctor," he told her. He would have suggested it even if she looked fine, but, at the moment, she didn't.

"You have…one of those…with you, too? In… your…pocket?" He was so resourceful, she thought, she wouldn't have put it past him. But he'd have to have big pockets…

"Not with me," he said wryly. "But in town, we do. We've got two of them, actually. They're both at the clinic," he told her. "Along with a couple of nurses. All really top-notch. They're certainly not in it for the money." He glanced over to the backseat. "Why don't I make you and Layla more comfortable in the backseat? There's more room to lie down there. And then I'll drive your truck into town."

Even if she'd wanted to protest, she didn't have the strength to do so. Devon felt way too tired.

"Whatever...you...say."

It was the last thing she recalled saying to the man who had come to her aid. In the next moment, every-thing suddenly and dramatically turned pitch-black.

She lost her hold on the world.

"Ma'am?" Cody asked uncertainly when he saw that she had shut her eyes. He got no response. "Devon?" he questioned more urgently, seeing her head nod to one side.

The next second, he quickly took the baby from her. Devon's hold had gone lax. The baby would have fallen if he hadn't moved fast.

"Damn," he mumbled. "New plan, Layla. We buckle your mom in where she is in the front seat and I drive into town, holding you in one arm. That okay with you?" He added under his breath, "Good thing Connor was always on us to multitask."

Getting out of the cab with the baby in his arms, Cody came around to the other side of the passenger seat to secure the seat belt as best he could around the unconscious woman.

He continued to talk to the baby, keeping his voice

at a soothing level, the way he did when he worked with spooked horses or cattle.

"Connor's my big brother. You'd like him. He's kind of bossy, but he had to be. He stuck around to raise my brother and sister and me when our dad died. Our mom died some years before that. Old Connor, he always came through." As he talked, he found that the sound of his voice was not just keeping the baby calm, but it was helping to do the same for him.

This wasn't exactly something that was covered in his deputy's manual. He was fairly certain that as far as his duties went, this was all brand-new ground he was crossing.

Slipping the metal tongue into the seat belt receptacle, he secured it. When he looked to make sure it would hold, that was when he became aware of the blood. There was a great deal more of it than there had been just a few minutes ago when Devon was struggling to push out her daughter.

Adrenaline spiked all through his veins. This was serious. *Really* serious.

He had to get this woman a doctor and fast or the baby in his arms was going to be an orphan before the sun set.

It took him a split second to make another decision. Running around to the rear of the truck, still holding the baby, Cody untied his horse. If he drove into town at a normal pace, the horse could easily keep up. But this was now a race for time. He intended to go as fast as he could. If still attached, the horse would be dragged in the truck's wake.

He spared the stallion one look and shouted a command. "Follow the truck, Flint. Follow the truck! Town, Flint. Town."

Telling his stallion the destination—a command he'd given often enough, except then it had been from the vantage point of a saddle astride the horse's back—he raced around to the driver's side and got in.

He didn't expect Flint to keep up, but, with luck, the horse would follow and reach town sometime after he did. If the horse didn't reach town by the time Cody would be able to look around for him, at least he knew that Flint wouldn't just run off aimlessly. Cody had spent long hours training the stallion. He was completely confident that, since the terrain was familiar to both of them, the horse would eventually find its way to Forever.

Climbing into the cab, still holding on to the baby who was now whimpering, Cody awkwardly buckled himself in. A quick check told him that, mercifully, Devon had left the keys in the ignition.

He started the truck, stepped on the gas and they were off.

Driving with one hand while holding the baby against him with his free arm proved to be tricky and definitely not something Cody had ever even *remotely* prepared for. But he didn't have the luxury of doubting that he was up to it or of looking around for an alternative method. There was no time for any of that. A woman's life—Layla's mother's life—depended on him being able to handle both the emergency and the baby.

Cody felt like he was running out of time.

He spared Devon an apprehensive glance. She was

still unconscious, but he did see her chest rising and falling. At least she was still breathing.

"You hang in there, you hear me?" he ordered Devon. How could he have missed that she was still bleeding? How could he not have seen all that blood soaking through her dress? he upbraided himself. "I've never lost a mother after she gave birth to her calf and I sure as hell don't intend to start with you."

Cody stepped down harder on the gas. He could see Flint trying to keep up in the rearview mirror, but the stallion was falling behind.

"I've got a feeling that you're all this little girl has, so don't even think of checking out. You're going to live, you understand? You're going to live! We're almost there," he told her, saying anything and everything that came into his head.

If he stopped talking, he was sure he was going to lose Devon.

"The town's just over that hill. It's not all that much to look at, but Forever's got really good people. People who take you in and look out for you. They don't care what your story is—although Miss Joan'll ask. Miss Joan, that's the woman who runs the diner. She's like a mother to all of us. Acts all grumpy, but she's got a heart as big as the state. She'll make sure you're warm and fed—she did with the four of us after our dad died. Did it so that it didn't seem like charity because Connor, he wouldn't have accepted any charity. *Ever*," Cody said. "He's way too proud. But Miss Joan, she always found a way to get around that. She'll just melt when she sees this baby of yours, even if she tries not to show it. And she'll give you advice you'll think you don't need—but you will."

The road ahead was wide open and empty. One hand clutching the steering wheel, he allowed himself to look in Devon's direction.

She was still unconscious. Her head was moving ever so slightly because of the vibrations caused by the increased speed.

Fear clawed at him. Fear that he wasn't going to make it to the clinic in time.

"You're not going to die, you hear me?" he told her. "I've never filled out a death report because of someone dying on my watch and I'm not going to start now. They're too long. They've got to be at least nine, ten pages long. You can't put me through that after I helped to deliver your baby, you hear me?"

Pushing down on the accelerator as hard as he could, he saw the outskirts of Forever rushing closer to him. It was just up ahead, within reach.

And then he breeched the city limits.

Keeping an eye out for any pedestrians and other cars, both of which were scarce, Cody tore straight through the center of Forever. The next moment, he was passing the town square, where the annual Christmas tree was always displayed.

Veering to the right and then to left, he didn't slow down until he reached his destination.

He practically put his foot through the floor as he pushed down on the brake as hard as he could.

The tires screeched in high-pitched protest as they came to a halt inches away from the front of the clinic.

## Chapter Three

As usual, the waiting room of Forever's lone medical clinic was very close to filled. It was the only available medical facility for fifty miles and the people of Forever were grateful for that. It wasn't all that long ago that the clinic had stood empty, its last physician having moved away thirty years ago. There was something comforting about having someone to turn to because they felt ill, or just because a husband or wife had nagged them into availing themselves of an annual—or bi-annual—exam.

Startled by the combined, unnerving sound of screeching tires and squealing brakes, everyone in the clinic's waiting room turned in unison toward the noise. As a rule, Forever was thought of by its residents as a sleepy little town that no one outside of the area ever really noticed and where nothing of consequence ever happened.

That meant that no one, either out of boredom or a sense of competitiveness, engaged in car races or harrowing displays of one-upmanship.

So when the teeth-jarring noise pierced the morning air, every patient within the waiting room, as well as the one nurse manning the desk, Debi White Eagle, instantly glanced in the direction of the bay window. The window looked out toward the front of the clinic.

"What the hell was that?"

Rancher Steven Hollis jumped to his feet, verbalizing what everyone else in the room was thinking.

The question didn't go unanswered for more than a couple of quick beats. Almost immediately thereafter, the roomful of patients witnessed what all would have readily agreed was a very unlikely sight: a bare-chested Deputy Cody McCullough bursting into the clinic with what appeared to be a newborn baby in his arms. The baby was wrapped in his uniform shirt.

Debi, a surgical nurse by vocation as well as one of the most recent additions to Forever's population, vacated her desk and rushed over to Cody.

"What happened?" she asked.

Cody quickly transferred Layla into her arms. "The baby's mother is in the truck. She's lost a lot of blood and I need help."

"Holly!" Debi yelled over her shoulder toward the rear of the clinic. "We need a doctor out here, STAT!"

It was an order she was accustomed to issuing when she worked at the hospital in Chicago. Here, however, the word left more than one of the patients looking at the others in bewilderment.

Grabbing the fresh lab coat she'd brought in for one of the doctors, Debi quickly removed Cody's shirt from around the tiny body and rewrapped the newborn in the lab coat. Acting in the interest of practicality, not to mention cleanliness, she figured the doctor would forgive her.

"Here," she said, giving Cody back his shirt. "You don't want to be out of uniform, Deputy."

With that, Debi immediately turned toward the most maternal patient available to her, Anita Moretti, who had five children and a brood of grandchildren of her own. "Anita, hold the baby," she requested, then looked at Cody. "Where's the mother?"

"Out here." He threw the words over his shoulder as, shrugging back into his shirt, he ran outside, secretly almost afraid of what he would see once he opened the truck's passenger door.

"Where is she?"

The question came from Dan Davenport, the doctor who had initially reopened the clinic and who was currently in charge of it as well as the care of the citizens of Forever.

Cody was already at the truck. He threw open the passenger door and unbuckled the seat belt that was the only thing holding Devon in place and semi-upright.

As carefully as he could, he lifted Devon out of the vehicle. The lower half of her dress was soaked with her blood.

Dan attempted to take the unconscious woman from him, but Cody shook his head. He wasn't about to let her go. "No, I've got her."

"This way," Dan said needlessly as he and Debi went back into the clinic ahead of Cody. "What happened?" Dan asked. "Did you find her this way?"

More than a dozen set of eyes looked in their direction as Cody carried the woman in.

"No, she was conscious and screaming when I found her," Cody answered, giving no indication that he even saw the other people in the room.

"Was she still in labor or had she given birth already?" Dan asked, leading the way to the room where he and his partner, Dr. Alisha Cordell-Murphy, performed both the simple surgeries and the ones that were classified as emergencies.

"As far as I could see, she had just started," Cody told him, aware that every word was being greedily absorbed by all the people in the waiting room. "I tried to help her. When she gave birth, I thought she'd be okay," Cody went on. "I didn't realize..." His voice drifted off helplessly.

It was clear to Dan by Cody's tone that he felt guilty that the situation had somehow devolved to this point.

"Not your fault," Dan told him, indicating the freshly prepared gurney in the room. "People don't realize that there are a lot of unforeseeable elements that can go wrong as a baby's being born."

"What have we got here?" Alisha Cordell-Murphy asked, peering into the room in response to Holly's summons. Her eyes widened when she saw the unconscious woman. "Omigod, who is she?" she asked, looking from Dan to the man who was covered in the woman's blood. She had only been in Forever a little over a year now, but she was acquainted—at least by sight—with everyone who lived within the area. This one was definitely not anyone she knew.

"Cody found her and brought her in," Dan answered.

Cody gave her the highlights. "Her truck was pulled over on the side of the road. I wouldn't have even seen it if she hadn't screamed," he confessed.

"I need plasma," Dan declared. "It looks like she's lost more blood than she can afford to."

Debi, who had come into the room with them, was cutting away the woman's clothing, preparing to put a sterile gown on her. Holly, who had already brought in the plasma, was now wordlessly preparing what she assumed the doctors were going to need to stop the hemorrhaging as well as to get a transfusion going.

Cody took a step back, and then another, giving everyone else there room to work. He felt as if he was just in the way.

"I'll just wait outside," he said to no one in particular as he took another step back.

Dan looked up, sparing him a fraction of a moment. "Don't go too far away. I've got a few more questions you might be able to answer."

"I don't know more than I just told you, but sure, I'll just be in the waiting room," Cody told the doctor, but he knew he was talking to himself. Everyone else in the room was busy, doing their best to try to save the woman's life.

Concerned and more than a little agitated, Cody slipped out.

The minute he was back in the waiting room, a barrage of questions rose all around him, coming from all different directions.

"You know her?"

"Where'd you find her?"

"Is this her baby?"

"Where's the father?"

There were more, all mingling with one another until it was just a huge wall of sound.

"Everyone, hush," Anita Moretti scolded, raising her voice to be heard above the rest. She was still holding the baby and rocking her as she patted the baby's bottom, doing her best to soothe the infant the way she had with each one of her children and grandchildren in turn. "Can't you people see that he's been through a lot, too?" Turning toward Cody, Mrs. Moretti smiled at him, the perennial, protective mother. "Don't pay them any mind, Cody. They're just looking for something exciting to talk about over dinner tonight. You don't have to say anything if you don't want to."

"There's not much to talk about," Cody told her, taking a seat and glancing around at the others. He was grateful for the woman's concern, but he was also very familiar with and understood a small-town mentality, especially since he'd become one of Sheriff Rick Santiago's deputies. "I was running late and only noticed the truck on the side of the road when I heard screams coming from it."

"She was on the side of the road?" Wade Hollister, one of the patients, asked.

Cody humored the man, despite the fact that he felt the answer was self-evident. "Well, she was in labor so I don't think she really felt like she was able to do any driving."

Rusty Saunders scratched his head. "Hell, what was she doing out there in her condition, anyway?"

Cody laughed quietly as he eased Layla out of Mrs. Moretti's arms. The woman looked at him skeptically, and then smiled and surrendered her precious package.

"I didn't get a chance to ask her," he told Rusty. "I was kind of busy at the time. We both were."

To underscore his point, he smiled at the baby in his arms.

"You delivered that?" Nathan McLane asked Cody. He was as close as possible to a permanent occupant at the Murphy brothers' saloon. His weathered expression was creased with awe.

Cody had never been one to embellish on a story or give himself credit if he could avoid it. He shrugged now. "I was just there to catch her. She more or less delivered herself," he told Nathan and the rest of the waiting-room occupants.

Travis Wakefield, ever the practical man, was obviously trying to work out the logistics to Cody's story. He'd gone to the window to look again at the truck Cody had driven over.

"You leave your truck back there?" he asked. "'Cause the one out there sure isn't yours."

That was when Cody suddenly remembered. He looked up. "My horse."

"What about Flint?" Red Yakima asked, getting up and moving closer to Cody.

Cody had risen to his feet as well and now walked over to the bay window, scanning as much of the area as he could make out from his present vantage point. Flint was nowhere in sight.

"I couldn't tie him to the back of the truck because I had to drive fast," he told Red. "I told him to follow me."

"You 'told' him to follow," Rosie Ortiz, one of the occupants in the waiting room, repeated skeptically. "And what, he said, 'Sure'?"

"Horses are smarter than most people," Red tonelessly informed the woman. He turned his attention back to Cody. "You want me to go out and see if I can find him for you?" the man offered.

Cody turned the matter over in his head. He could either take the man up on his offer or turn the infant back over to Mrs. Moretti—and he did want to hang around to make sure Devon pulled through. There was a chance that she might not, although he really didn't want to entertain that idea for the baby's sake.

He had no idea why, but he felt that if he remained here, she wouldn't die. He knew he was being superstitious, but everyone around here had some superstition they clung to. His was that if he walked out, the door would be left open for bad things to transpire.

Cody looked at the weathered ranch hand he had known for most of his life. "I'd appreciate that, Red."

"Don't mention it," the man told him, waving a dismissive hand. "I'll stop at the sheriff's office and tell them you didn't fall into a ditch or off the side of the cliff, put Rick's mind at ease," Red added matter-of-factly.

"I owe you."

Red smiled for the first time. "Hey, buy me a beer next time we're at the saloon together and we'll call it even."

"You got it," Cody agreed, although in his opinion it didn't really even begin to repay the man for taking the trouble to track Flint down.

Red walked out of the clinic.

Less than a minute later, Holly came out, an apologetic expression on her face. She looked around the waiting room at the patients.

"It's going to be a while, I'm afraid," she told them. Braced for complaints, she was surprised when none were voiced. "The doctors have got their hands full. Your names are all on the sign-in sheet. If you'd like to come back tomorrow, you'll be seen in the order that you arrived today," she said, once again looking around the room, waiting for some sort of descent or grumbling.

"How long is 'a while'?" Oral Hanson wanted to know, obviously weighing his options.

Holly answered honestly. "At least a couple of hours." Honesty forced her to add, "Maybe more."

The man shrugged his wide shoulder. "Got nothin' I'm doing anyway, not since my boys took over the ranch. Seems they're always telling me to 'go take a load off' anyway, so I might as well do that and stay put." Smiling at the baby in Cody's arms, he added, "I'd like to find out if the little one's mama pulls through."

Most of the other patients were not of the same mind as Oral. They had busy lives to get back to, so they decided to leave the clinic and return the next day as suggested.

But a few, including Mrs. Moretti, remained. When Cody looked at the older woman quizzically, Mrs. Moretti said, "I thought maybe I'd stick around, give you a little help if you need it. You'll want to have your hands free if they call you back in there." Lowering her voice, she added, "You know, just in case."

It was obvious to Cody that Mrs. Moretti had already convinced herself that there was more going on between him and the woman he'd found today.

Anita Moretti wasn't a gossip by any stretch of the imagination, but the woman did enjoy a good story, both hearing one and, occasionally, passing one along. He couldn't fault her for being human, even though what he knew she was thinking was entirely a fabrication.

And Cody knew better than to protest or try to set the woman straight. Saying anything to the contrary would only get him more deeply entrenched. Mrs. Moretti would go on believing what she chose to believe.

Connor had always maintained that when you lost control of the situation, the best thing to do was to politely say "thank you" and then back away as quickly as possible.

"I appreciate that, Mrs. Moretti," Cody told the woman.

Because he was agitated and didn't know what to do with himself, Cody began to walk the floor. Layla seemed to enjoy the rhythmic movements and before long obligingly dozed off.

Making no secret of the fact that she was watching him, Mrs. Moretti smiled and gave him the thumbs-up. "You're a natural," she told Cody, beaming.

"I'm not doing anything but walking," Cody pointed out.

He heard the door behind him opening. Turning, he was about to tell whomever had come in that service was temporarily on hold until further notice.

But he didn't have to say anything. It wasn't a new patient. Red had returned to the clinic.

"Couldn't find Flint?" Cody asked the older man. Red hadn't been gone very long, but, then, Cody had no right to expect him to scour the area. After all, Flint belonged to him, not Red.

"Didn't really have to look," Red replied. "That is one loyal stallion you've got yourself there, Mc-

Cullough. Saw him coming right into the outskirts of town, as pretty as you please, minding his own business like he didn't have a care in the world and was just out for a morning stroll. Had to gentle him a little before I tied him to the hitching post down the street, but that's to be expected. He's waiting for you there," the ranch hand informed him.

Well, that was a relief, Cody thought. He hadn't realized he was so concerned until just this moment. He supposed this morning's events had stretched his nerves taut to the very limit.

"I appreciate it," Cody told the man.

"Yeah, yeah," Red dismissed the words of gratitude. "I said a beer would square us, remember? Now I'll go tell the sheriff you're safe and sound. See you around, McCullough," he told Cody.

Inclining his head in a show of respect, Red nodded at Mrs. Moretti just before he left the clinic.

## Chapter Four

As Cody tried to decide his next move, the infant he was holding against him began to make a noise he couldn't quite make out. It didn't exactly sound like a whimper or a cry, but the baby was definitely voicing some sort of discontent.

In a few seconds, he had his answer. The infant had turned her head into his chest and appeared to be rooting around, her tiny lips making noises as she attempted to suck on his shirt.

"Looks like she's hungry," Mrs. Moretti told him helpfully. "She's trying to get her sustenance out of your shirt."

"Sorry, Layla, I'm afraid you're out of luck there," Cody told the baby, very gently separating the tiny mouth from his shirt.

At a temporary loss as to what to do, he looked at Mrs. Moretti for help.

The older woman shook her head. "I'm afraid I don't have anything for her. I stopped carrying formula with me several years ago. All my grandchildren are older than she is. But let me see if I can get one of the nurses to find something for her."

Rising heavily to her feet, the woman approached

the registration desk and looked over it in hopes of seeing someone coming out of the impromptu operating room. She didn't, but that didn't stop her.

Making her way around the desk, Mrs. Moretti continued to the rear of the clinic. The doors to four of the exam rooms were wide open. Mrs. Moretti zeroed in on the one that was closed. When Melissa, one of her granddaughters, had needed stitches for the gash she'd gotten on her forehead thanks to a game of hide-and-seek that had gone wrong, she'd been taken into that room.

Knocking on the door, Mrs. Moretti raised her voice. "Sorry to bother you, but the baby out here seems to be hungry. Is there any formula in the clinic?" she asked politely.

After a moment the door opened in response to Mrs. Moretti's question. Holly was in the doorway.

"You didn't have to come out, dear. You could have just told me where the formula's kept and I would have gotten it," the woman said to Holly.

If given a choice, Mrs. Moretti always preferred being self-sufficient instead of dependent on the help of others.

"It's just easier this way," Holly told the woman. Besides, the doctors really didn't want to have civilians rooting through their supplies. However, there was no polite way to say that to Mrs. Moretti, so she let that pass. "How's everyone out here?" she asked as she took the woman to the supply cabinet in the last exam room.

There were several bottles of formula on the bottom shelf. Taking one, Holly decided to look in on the baby before heating the formula up.

"Mostly gone," Mrs. Moretti told her matter-of-factly, still following behind her. "Except for a couple of us. And, of course, Cody and the baby. Poor little thing's *hungry*." She smiled sympathetically. "I guess being born was hard work for her."

"I guess so," Holly agreed. She walked out into the waiting room. "How's our girl?" she asked Cody.

He was rocking the baby back and forth in an attempt to soothe her. "Okay, I think." And then he flushed. "I've got more experience with newborn calves than humans."

It amazed Holly how someone who looked the way Cody McCullough did—broad-shouldered, athletic with a soft, sexy smile and soul-melting blue eyes—could be so humble.

"You're doing fine, Cody," she assured him. "I'll just go and warm up this formula for you." Holly paused for a moment, needing to ask him a question just to be sure. "You all right with feeding it to her?"

Cody nodded, adding, "Not much different than with a calf, right?"

She'd never heard it put quite that way before. She supposed that there were similarities. "As long as you make sure you don't try to get her to stand up while she's doing it."

Cody laughed. "I think I've already figured that part out."

HOLLY RETURNED WITHIN MINUTES, the small bottle of formula warmed and ready to be given to the hungry infant. "There you go," she said, handing Cody the bottle.

She was about to coach him through it, but saw

that she needn't have worried. Cody was doing just fine with feeding the baby.

Instead, she gave him an encouraging smile. Still, she had to admit to herself that there was a little concern on her part.

"You're sure you'll be all right out here?" she asked him.

"He'll be fine," Mrs. Moretti told the nurse, answering for Cody. "I'll stay on just in case," she volunteered.

Cody looked at the older woman as he fed Layla. "You sure? It might be a long wait to see one of the doctors, when they're finally free."

It was becoming obvious that the delay would be even longer than anticipated. "I can come back for that tomorrow, but I'll stay here with you as long as you feel I might be of some help."

"I don't want to keep you, Mrs. Moretti," Cody told her.

Mrs. Moretti laughed. "It's been a long time since I was a kept woman," she told him with a wink that both surprised and amused him. There was still a little bit of the young flirt within the older matron. And then she waved her hand, dismissing his protest. "Don't give it another thought."

Feeling that everything was under control, Holly told them, "I'd better be getting back in there."

A flash of anxiety came out of nowhere, surprising Cody. "How is she doing?" he asked.

"Better than when you first brought her in." That was all Holly felt comfortable saying at this point. She'd learned that it was better to say too little than too much.

With that, the young nurse left the waiting room and hurried back to the operating room.

Mrs. Moretti sensed Cody's concern.

"She'll be fine," she assured Cody, patting his hand in the same soothing fashion she'd employed with all of her own children. "They don't come any better than Dr. Dan and Dr. Alisha," the grandmother of six told him. "Those two are the best thing that ever happened to this little town," she said with conviction.

HALF AN HOUR PASSED. Layla finished the formula that Holly had brought out for her.

Though he strained his ears, Cody couldn't discern anything coming from the rear of the clinic. He didn't hear any voices, nor did he hear a door being opened.

This "operation" was going on much too long, he thought. Something was very wrong.

As if reading his mind, Mrs. Moretti leaned forward. Her eyes meeting his, she told him, "Remember, no news is good news."

"Yeah," he murmured without conviction.

Cody knew that the woman meant well, but the old saying didn't really comfort him at this point. He'd always been the kind of person who met everything head-on. He didn't have that option here. All he could do was wait and the inactivity was making him fidget inwardly.

"Well, I guess I'll come back tomorrow," Oral Hanson suddenly announced to the room, even though Cody and Mrs. Moretti were the only two occupants left.

After getting up, the man crossed over and paused

in front of Cody. He looked down at the baby and allowed a nostalgic expression to pass over his face.

"Brings back memories," he explained, referring to when his children had been that small. "You hang in there, Cody, you hear?"

Cody merely nodded. There wasn't anything else that he could do, really.

"You're doing a good thing," Oral said as he left the clinic.

"He's right, you know," Mrs. Moretti told Cody, adding her voice to the sentiment.

He was *really* beginning to feel guilty having the woman remain here with him.

"Mrs. Moretti, you don't have to stay any longer," he told her. "You've got a family to get back to."

He knew that because of extenuating circumstances, Mrs. Moretti was helping to raise two of her younger grandchildren. It wasn't fair to the woman to make her stay on his account. After all, it wasn't as if he was helpless.

But Mrs. Moretti shook her head. "I don't feel right about leaving you alone."

"Two doctors and two nurses is not 'alone,' Mrs. Moretti," he reminded her. "All I have to do is raise my voice and one of them is bound to come out. Really, go home to your family," he urged, then added, "Layla and I will be fine. Really."

Mrs. Moretti's dark eyes crinkled as she smiled at the sleeping infant in his arms. "Such a lovely name," she told him. "That was your mama's name, wasn't it?" she asked. Cody nodded in response. "All right," the older woman said with a resigned sigh as she rose to her feet. "I guess they'll be wondering what happened to me if I don't get home soon." Mrs. Moretti spared him one last encouraging pat on the shoulder. "Don't give up hope, Cody."

"No, ma'am, I won't," he promised her.

Nodding her head, Mrs. Moretti picked up her oversize purse and finally made her way out of the clinic.

"Looks like it's just you and me now," Cody whispered to the baby once the door had closed behind Mrs. Moretti.

"And then," he amended as he heard the door to the clinic opening again, "maybe not." Raising his voice so that the woman would turn around, Cody said, "Mrs. Moretti, really, it's okay. Go home."

"I'm not Mrs. Moretti and I'm not going home, at least not until I find out just what the hell is going on here."

Surprised, holding the baby pressed against his chest, Cody shifted around in his seat to see Connor walking into the clinic.

Anyone looking at them would have instantly known that Cody and Connor were brothers, but Connor, three years older and two inches taller, was leaner and more weathered-looking than Cody. And while they both had the same blue eyes, Connor's hair was a darker shade of blond than Cody's.

"Where did you get that?" Connor asked, nodding at the baby as he took a seat next to his brother.

"Mrs. Abernathy was having a yard sale," Cody cracked. "I couldn't help myself."

"I'll let that go," Connor told him. He studied his brother for a moment. "I hear that you've had a hard morning."

"Exactly what did you hear?" Cody asked. Because the infant was reacting to the sound of Connor's deep voice, Cody began to rock her gently.

The reaction did not do unnoticed by Connor, though he made no comment. "Well, your truck's still where you parked it last night and your horse is missing, so I figured out that the damn thing wouldn't start—the truck, not the horse. And then there's your little midwife adventure."

"Who told you?" Cody asked. Connor had been out mending fences early this morning. How had his brother heard about any of this? he wondered.

Connor grinned. "You know that Rusty Saunders never could keep anything to himself for more than five minutes. He rode out to the ranch to tell me. I gather the thought of you as a midwife tickled him pink."

Cody blew out a breath as he shook his head. "Man always was easily entertained."

"Yeah, well, it doesn't take much for some," Connor agreed. "I brought you a change of clothes," he said to Cody. "I figured after the way he described you, you'd need it." Giving his brother the once over—Cody was still wearing the bloodied shirt he'd had on when he carried Devon into the clinic—Connor nodded. "Looks like he wasn't wrong."

He put the brown paper sack containing a clean shirt and jeans down on the floor next to his brother's feet. "So, that's the little one, huh?" he asked, softening marginally as he gazed at the infant. The next moment, he looked up at his brother, the expression on his face that of a man who felt vindication. "See, I always said helping out during calving season would come in handy for you someday."

Cody nodded. He knew better than to question his brother's memory. Besides, Connor probably had said something like that at one time or another. "That's what you told me."

"How's her mother?" Connor asked.

"I don't know," Cody told him honestly. "Nobody's really told me anything since the two docs got to work on her."

The words were simple, but Connor heard his brother's concern. Not that he expected Cody to be aloof, but there was a tad more feeling in Cody's tone than Connor was accustomed to hearing.

"They're good people" was all Connor said of the doctors by way of encouragement. Still, the implied endorsement spoke volumes. "You need anything?" Connor asked, getting ready to leave.

"Not me. But she might do with a miracle," he told Connor, nodding back toward the rear of the clinic, where the door to the fifth exam room was still closed.

"I figure that part was already covered when you showed up." Connor started to rise, then abruptly stopped. "I can stick around if you want," he offered.

Cody laughed. "You don't do 'sticking around' well and you know it. Leave you in one place for too long and you'll be climbing right out of your skin. Thanks for coming."

Connor merely shrugged off his brother's thanks. "Flint's at the hitching post down the street a ways," he told Cody.

"I know. He's a good horse. He followed me to

town behind the truck." Proud of the animal, Cody felt he had to share that with Connor. "Red found him for me."

"Good man, Red. Well, I'll see you when I see you," Connor said on his way to the door. One hand on the doorknob, he paused just before leaving. "Want Cassidy to come by?" he asked.

"And have my ear talked off?" Cody laughed. "No, I've got this covered."

Connor nodded. "I figured you did." And, with that, he walked out, closing the door behind him.

THE BABY HAD dozed off again and slept in his arms. For a while, there was nothing but the sound of her breathing to keep him company. Cody kept glancing toward the rear of the clinic, but the door didn't open. It felt as if he was doomed to wait in vain forever.

And then, just as he had given up all hope, Cody heard the door finally open.

For a moment, he thought he'd imagined it. Even so, he anxiously rose to his feet. And then he heard voices. Happy voices, not agitated ones.

Within a minute, Dan walked out to the front of the clinic. He looked somewhat tired, but he definitely had the air of a man who had won the battle he'd fought.

"Is she all right?"

The words burst from Cody's lips before he even realized he was asking the question out loud.

Rather than answer one way or the other, Dan asked, "Why don't you go see for yourself?"

Cody didn't remember crossing the waiting room, didn't really remember Holly coming up to him to take the baby from his arms. And he was only marginally aware of the fact that his arms ached from having held the baby in that position for so long.

All he knew was that Dan was leading him into the room where a battle to save a woman's life had been fought—and won.

When he walked in, Devon's eyes were closed. No longer on the surgical gurney, she had been transferred onto the lone hospital bed the clinic had.

An uneasiness began to take hold of Cody as he drew closer to her.

She still looked so pale, he thought.

Apprehension came out of some dark, hidden place, drenching Cody as he asked Dan, "Is she—is she—she's not—is she?"

He had lived through a lot in his time—the death of first one parent, then the other, the possibility of having the family split up and winding up in foster care. But even with all that, Cody couldn't make himself say the words.

Dan, who had lost his only brother just before he came to Forever, empathized. He put a wide, comforting hand on the younger man's shoulder as he told him, "She's alive, Cody. She's just sleeping."

The wave of relief surprised Cody as it all but knocked him off his feet.

## Chapter Five

Cody trusted the doctor and knew that Dr. Davenport wasn't about to mislead him or sugarcoat the situation. He just wanted to hear the doctor assure him again.

"She's just sleeping, Dr. Dan, right? You're sure about that?" Cody questioned.

Because if she wasn't, if she had somehow managed to slip away, no matter what anyone else said, Cody would feel that it was somehow his fault, that he had overlooked something and hadn't kept the woman safe.

"You know she's been through a lot," Dan tactfully reminded him. "Her being asleep is a good thing. The body does its best recuperative work when it's asleep. That way, it's only focused on that one thing."

Cody could buy that. But what if she remained that way? What if she never woke up? he worried. "How long do you think she'll, you know, be asleep?"

"She'll wake up when she's ready. Meanwhile, I'm going to have her stay here." Guessing Cody's next question, Dan added, "Don't worry. She won't be alone. I'll have someone stay with her."

Which was his euphemistic way of saying that *he*

would be that "someone." He knew his wife, Tina, wouldn't exactly be overjoyed about having him stay the night, but she had long ago made her peace with the fact that that sort of thing went with the territory and she was nothing if not supportive.

Cody never hesitated. He had made up his mind the moment the doctor said Devon was going to remain at the clinic overnight. "Can I be that someone?"

Dan looked at the deputy, surprised and a little skeptical. "You?"

Cody nodded. "I found her and I'd kind of like to see this through if you don't mind. It's something that Connor taught us was important—to finish something that you've started."

Dan nodded. "Well, I certainly can't argue with that." He made a quick assessment before giving Cody an answer. "Everything should be fine. But if she wakes up suddenly, or if you feel uneasy about how she's doing for *any reason at all, call me*," Dan ordered. "I'm only five minutes away." That was the advantage of living in town instead of on one of the outlying ranches, as both of his nurses did.

Cody was already pulling up a chair, positioning it beside the bed. "Thanks." And then he suddenly remembered—appalled that he could have forgotten, even for a moment. "The baby—" he began, looking around as if he expected the infant to be close by.

"—will be coming home with me," Dan informed him. "Nothing Tina likes better than to have a baby to fuss over." He could see that Cody was about to offer a protest. Like the rest of his family, the deputy obviously didn't know when to stop shouldering responsibility. "You'll have enough to do just watching over the baby's mother. By the way, Holly's going to need some information from you about the patient," he told Cody, nodding at the woman in the hospital bed.

"Can't help you there," Cody confessed. "I don't know much, just her first name. Devon."

Dan nodded. "It's a start. Listen, have you had anything to eat since this whole thing started?" he asked.

Cody shook his head. Food was the very last thing on his mind. He hadn't taken his eyes off Devon since he'd walked in and he really wished that the woman didn't look so pale.

"No."

Dan's eyes met the deputy's. "I can stay here and wait until you swing by the diner and get something to go," the doctor offered.

"That's okay, Doc. I'm good" he said, turning the doctor's offer down. "You've already done more than enough," Cody added gratefully.

Dan smiled, brushing off the thanks. "It's what I signed up for," he reminded the younger man.

It wasn't every doctor who felt morally bound to care this much. Despite the fact that they'd had to wait thirty years, everyone in town felt that they had really lucked out when Dr. Davenport reopened the clinic.

"Even so, she'd be dead by now if it weren't for you and Dr. Alisha," Cody said with all sincerity.

Dan smiled. Cody had forgotten one key point. It was so like the McCulloughs. "And don't forget you. If you hadn't found her and come to her aid, none of this would have been possible."

Dan paused for a moment to study the younger man's profile. Cody already appeared to have settled in for the night. He wasn't going anywhere.

"Okay, then," he said, resigned, "if you don't have any more questions, then I'm off. Remember, just five minutes away." He got a nod from Cody in response. The deputy's eyes were once again trained on the sleeping patient.

Dan took his cue and quietly slipped out of the room, leaving the door open.

"Who are you?" Cody asked the unconscious woman after a few minutes had passed and the clinic had slipped into stony silence, letting him know that everyone was gone. "And what kind of a man would have let you go, especially in your condition, carrying his baby?

"Unless he had a damn good reason for it, he should be horse-whipped if he shows up here, looking for you." Cody quickly amended, "Not that we whip our horses around here. But for someone like that guy, an exception could definitely be made.

"Come to think of it, I can't come up with *any* kind of a reason for him to have let you go off like that by yourself. The guy has to be dumber than a box of rocks—" he concluded "—and I'm probably insulting the rocks. I can see why you wouldn't want to be around him. More important—why you wouldn't want your baby to be around him. Babies need someone to look up to, to stimulate them. That sure doesn't sound like the man who let you go off by yourself."

Cody sighed, dragging his hand through his hair. He was at a loose end, not to mention somewhat confused. He felt like a man who had been on a roller coaster for too long, having taken both the uphill climb and the harrowing, steep plunge once too often.

In short, he knew he wasn't making any sense, but

all these emotions were suddenly popping up, rising to the surface like bubbles in a shaken soda can—dangerously ready to explode.

Cody struggled to get his emotions back in line. "You just take your time waking up," he told Devon. "Doc said you needed your rest and he should know. Until Doc Alisha came along, Dr. Dan had been taking care of the town on his own for a while now. Word has it that his brother was supposed to be the one coming to take care of us—first doctor in thirty years since the clinic closed—but the night before he was supposed to fly out, he was killed in a car accident, so Dr. Dan came in his place.

"I never knew the other Dr. Davenport, but speaking for the town, I'd say we got ourselves a really good deal, getting Dr. Dan."

Cody made himself as comfortable as he could as he continued talking to the woman he'd saved.

"And speaking *of* the town, you'll find that, if you decide to stay here a while, this is a really nice place, both for you and for your daughter. People here like to watch out for each other. It's the kind of thing that makes you feel safe and protected without feeling like you're confined or imprisoned. I should know. I'm a deputy sheriff—" he quickly clarified "—not that we imprison anyone."

His words and Devon's even breathing filled the silence. He went on talking, hoping that he could somehow comfort the woman. He'd read somewhere that people in comas responded to the sound of someone talking to them.

"Having a sheriff's department is just putting window dressing on the notion of a town," he said honestly. "Not that I don't like being a deputy," he went on, "but I would have done what I did this morning even if I was still just one of the ranchers around here." He confided, "As a deputy, I'm supposed to keep the peace, but mostly the peace keeps itself." Still, he liked the idea of being part of a law enforcement department in Forever.

"Did you get to the part about me yet?"

The raspy, honey-whiskey voice startled him. Cody twisted around in his seat to see Miss Joan standing behind him in the room. The thin redhead was holding a tray full of food.

"Miss Joan, I didn't see you there," Cody confessed, immediately jumping to his feet out of an ingrained sense of respect.

"Obviously. You probably also didn't hear what I just said," she assumed and then repeated it. "I asked if you'd gotten to me yet, seeing as how you're giving this poor, unconscious girl a verbal tour of the good citizens of Forever. Not fair," she judged, "since she can't get away."

"I just wanted her to know that she was safe," Cody explained philosophically.

Miss Joan set down the tray on the counter beside the sink that the medical staff used for washing up before procedures.

"Nothing wrong with that," she agreed. "I was going to have one of the girls bring this to you, but I decided to come myself."

He assumed that someone from the clinic, possibly Mrs. Moretti, had stopped by the diner to share what was going on with Miss Joan. Everyone knew that nothing ever seemed to take place in Forever without

Miss Joan somehow being aware of it. Aware and ultimately involved in her own way, she was thought by many to be the veritable heart of the town.

"You really didn't have to go to the trouble," Cody told her, even as the tempting aroma of fried chicken, mashed potatoes and green beans with bread crumbs filled the room.

"I did if I didn't want to have you on my conscience, sitting here, keeping vigil and slowly starving." Besides, she added silently, she wanted to see the young woman for herself.

Coming around closer to the bed, Miss Joan took her first good look at the young woman at the center of the little drama that had everyone in Forever talking.

"Pretty little thing," she pronounced. "Kind of young, too, to be out on her own this way."

Long-ago memories whispered across the frontier of her mind before Miss Joan shut them away.

Turning away from the young woman, Miss Joan looked at Cody. "You need anything?" she asked him in her take-charge tone that everyone was familiar with.

Cody looked at the tray. Miss Joan had even brought dessert. His favorite. Boston cream pie. Even though he knew the meal had been prepared by Angel, another one of the people Miss Joan had taken under her wing, the woman herself never ceased to amaze him. She somehow always instinctively managed to be there, filling needs no one had voiced.

"No, ma'am, I think you've taken care of everything as usual. Thanks," he told her. Sliding back on his chair so he could dig into the pocket of his jeans, he asked, "What do I owe you, Miss Joan?"

The withering glance the older woman gave him had Cody stop reaching for his money.

"We'll come to terms" was all she said. Everyone knew that she believed favors were to be paid forward. It was a given. "You know where she was heading?" Miss Joan asked.

Cody shook his head. "Haven't a clue, ma'am."

"Well, if she decides that she doesn't want to keep on going there for some reason, let her know that I could always use another girl at my place once she gets up on her feet," Miss Joan told him. "And she'll need somewhere to stay," she added, stating the obvious.

The town had a new hotel—their only one—but hotels were expensive.

Cody suppressed a sigh as he turned back to look at the sleeping young woman. "First, she needs to wake up," he said more to himself than to Miss Joan.

Miss Joan nodded. "First things first," she agreed. It was time to leave. Miss Joan made a point of never staying longer than she felt necessary. "Don't let that get cold," she told him, nodding at the food on the tray she'd brought.

Cody was already drawing his chair over to the tray. When he glanced up to thank her again, he realized that Miss Joan had gone.

Smiling to himself, he began to eat, discovering only then just how hungry he actually was.

CODY SAVED SOME of the food that Miss Joan had brought, just in case Devon woke up hungry. But the hours passed and the young woman continued sleeping.

Reminding himself that the doctor had told him this was a good thing—and checking on Devon a couple more times to assure himself that she was breathing—Cody finally settled back in the chair he'd relocated by her bed. Within minutes, he fell into a light, uneasy sleep.

FRAGMENTS OF DREAMS kept collecting, then colliding and ultimately breaking apart in her head. They were all different from one another, but they still had one thing in common.

They were all dreams that revolved around being lost. Hopelessly lost. Lost in the desert, lost in an amusement park, lost in a large city, lost in a school she remembered from her childhood. In each instance, for however long or short that particular dream fragment lasted, she was trying to find her way home, trying to find something she had lost besides herself. Though, in the scope of the dream, she had no idea what it was that she was looking for or even exactly where this "home" was.

Or even *if* it was home.

All she was aware of was this urgent need within her to find it.

It felt as if it went on for hours, this odyssey-without-end that she was on, going from dream to unsettling dream. A few times, as the kaleidoscope of locations kept changing, she somehow felt that she was close to journey's end only to have home suddenly disappear, leaving her stranded. And then the so-called adventure began again, taking on a new scenario, but accompanied by the same feeling.

Eternally lost, Devon felt exhausted, frightened and incredibly sweaty as she continued trudging to nowhere. A despondency began to eat away at her, making her feel as if she was in some kind of a loop, a loop that kept sending her through the motions of this search-without-a-solution over and over again.

Somewhere in her dream, Devon came to realize that the baby that had literally been a part of her for so long was missing, abruptly taken away from her very body. The sense of urgency to find the infant, to find *home* increased exponentially. She strained to wake herself up, somehow sensing that if she could just do that one thing, if she could succeed in waking herself up, then this futile search would be over and her baby would be returned to her.

She tried to cry out, to somehow rise above the downward pull that was attempting to submerge her once and for all.

Opening her mouth, she felt water rushing into it, threatening to drown her. She had no idea where it had come from, but if she wanted to remain alive, she knew she was supposed to close her mouth. But if she did that, then she couldn't wake herself up and, eventually, that would completely suffocate her.

Feeling she had no choice, afraid that retreating would ultimately lead to her baby's demise somehow, Devon opened her mouth and screamed, even as water once again came rushing in to silence her.

She screamed again, louder—and finally, just before drowning, succeeded in waking herself up.

She woke up looking at the sky.

No, not the sky. She was looking into the bluest eyes she'd ever seen.

And she wasn't drowning anymore.

# Chapter Six

Cody had just managed to doze off, despite his best efforts not to. In this case, although he was generally a light sleeper, he had somehow fallen into a deep sleep. So much so that the screams he heard initially incorporated themselves into his dream and, suddenly, he was back in Devon's truck, doing his level best to help her bring her daughter into the world.

But because he was always so logical, even when asleep, something nudged at Cody's consciousness, making him realize that the scenario he believed himself in was all wrong.

They had both been through this already. Devon had already given birth to the baby and, since she'd only been pregnant with one child, this couldn't possibly be real no matter what it felt like.

She couldn't be giving birth again.

But the scream was very real, so there had to be another reason for it.

Devon was in trouble.

Sheer will and almost military discipline forced Cody to wake up. He did so with a start.

The second he did, he was up on his feet and beside Devon's bed. A railing was all that separated them and Cody hardly noticed it. He hovered over Devon, wanting to wake her up. The only thing that stopped him was that he'd once read that it was bad to wake up someone who was sleepwalking.

The moment's hesitation evaporated as he reminded himself that she was *not* sleepwalking, she was obviously in the throes of some kind of nightmare.

Before Cody could put his hand on her shoulder to rouse her, Devon's eyes flew open. He saw fear mingling with confusion within the deep blue orbs.

But what he also saw—and what seemed to grow at nearly lightning speed—was relief.

"It's you," she breathed. Devon felt as if she was still gasping for air. She struggled to tamp down the sense of panic.

"It is," he replied, only hoping that she wasn't mistaking him for the low-life scum who had allowed this woman to be out on the open road by herself.

The look of relief on her face gave way to concern as Devon attempted to prop herself up on her elbows while looking around the room at the same time.

"Hey, you're supposed to be lying back and resting," Cody insisted, gently putting a restraining hand on her shoulder. "Don't exert yourself."

"My baby," Devon cried. Still scanning the area as if she'd somehow missed seeing the baby in the small room the first around. "Where's my baby?" There was panic in her eyes as she clutched Cody's arm. "She's not—"

It didn't take much to guess at what Devon wasn't saying.

"Oh no, no, she's fine," Cody reassured her. "She's better than fine. Layla's with Dr. Dan."

"Layla?" Devon repeated, bewildered, her brain still somewhat foggy. She was having trouble processing information. Nothing seemed to be making sense to her. "Dr. Dan?"

To Cody's relief, he began to see color returning to the young woman's cheeks. If she seemed addled, that was just because the last few hours of exertion had caused her to forget some things.

He backtracked. "Layla's what you decided to name the baby," he told her patiently. "And Dr. Dan's one of the two doctors at the clinic who saved your life. He lives in town. Dr. Dan thought it might be easier for you, as well as the baby, to have someone else take care of Layla while you just concentrate on getting better yourself." He saw that she was about to protest so he quickly pointed out, "By the time I got you to the clinic, you'd lost a lot of blood. You gave us all quite a scare."

Devon blinked, trying to absorb everything this man had just told her and make some kind of sense of it. It wasn't easy. Her brain felt like a giant piece of Swiss cheese with information falling through the holes. Devon looked at him more closely.

And then she remembered. "You're the guy who stopped."

Cody supposed that was as apt a description for him as any. Except that there was one important thing missing. "And the guy who delivered your baby," he added matter-of-factly.

It began coming back to her in large, all-encompassing chunks. Her eyes widened as she suddenly recalled his name. "You're Cody."

Sharing the moment with her, Cody felt almost triumphant.

"That's right." He leaned in a little closer to her. "How are you feeling?"

That was an easy one. She didn't even have to pause before answering his question.

"Like one of those Saturday-morning cartoon characters who was run over and flattened by a truck."

Cody laughed quietly. "There's a reason for that," he told her.

Devon eyed him warily, trying to understand. "You ran me over with a truck?"

Cody suppressed a grin. He didn't want her to think he was laughing at her. "No, but you did lose a lot of blood. That would explain why you feel the way you do now."

The room was well lit and Devon was able to focus on the man sitting beside her bed. There were streaks of blood evident along both halves of his tan uniform.

"Is that some of mine?" she asked, nodding at the blood.

Connor had brought him a change of clothes, but Cody hadn't wanted to leave her side long enough to change—and it didn't seem right to do it in her room, even though she *was* unconscious. After a bit, to be honest, he'd been too concerned about Devon to even think about his own appearance.

Looking down at himself now, he saw what Devon was seeing. There were streaks of blood, dried now, along the front of his shirt, as well as additional amounts, not nearly as pronounced, along his pants legs.

"Yes, it is. Sorry," he apologized. Getting up, he walked over to where he'd left his other clothes. Removing the bloodstained shirt, he switched into the clean one.

Devon's head was still spinning a little and there was no question that she felt pretty woozy, not to mention shaken. But, even factoring that in, Devon could still appreciate the fact that the person she was looking at was more than just a passably attractive man. He was the closest specimen to bone-melting gorgeousness she had ever seen. His solid muscles testified that he was a man who didn't allow others do his work for him but tackled head-on whatever came his way.

She caught herself wondering if those muscles felt as hard as they looked.

*Get a grip, Devon.*

"I can wash that for you," she told Cody, feeling somewhat guilty that he had gotten his clothes dirty on her account.

He flashed a quick smile of thanks even as he shook his head. "You're in no shape to do anything right now," he told her.

"I didn't mean right now," Devon protested. Right now, she doubted that she could even stand up. But she was determined to be better by tomorrow. "But when I get back on my feet… Where am I, anyway?" she asked suddenly, trying to look around again.

This time, she didn't try to sit up. Exhaustion prevented her from doing very much of anything but lying there. Still, she was able to take in her surrounding area, such as it was.

"This is the clinic I told you about earlier," he reminded her, doing his best to give her a sense of continuity. "The doctors have this room set aside for any emergency surgeries that might come in."

"Why not just have people go to the hospital?" she asked.

Cody shook his head. He had lived here all his life, so to him what the doctors did at the clinic wasn't unusual, but he knew that an outsider wouldn't see it that way.

"The closest hospital is fifty miles away," he told her. "A person can't always get there in time. It would be too dangerous to wait that long."

Devon took in a deep breath as the fact that she might have actually died today began to dawn on her. "Like me."

"Like you," Cody confirmed. He thought of the meal that Miss Joan had brought him. There was still a little of that left. Devon needed to eat something so she could build up her strength. "Are you hungry?" he asked.

The mere mention of food caused her stomach to bunch up and threaten to rise up in her throat.

"Oh Lord, no," Devon cried with feeling. Cody had already seen her close to naked, but she found the thought of throwing up in front of him extremely embarrassing. It took her a moment to catch her breath.

When she did, Devon asked him, "Did I say thank you yet?"

Without specifically answering her question, Cody

grinned and replied, "As I recall, you were kind of busy screaming and pushing."

That part was still rather a blur, with the events all running together into one murky whole.

Her eyes held this. "Then I'll say it now." Her voice softened. "Thank you."

Cody wasn't a man who felt comfortable in the face of gratitude, even though he appreciated the fact that she felt that way.

He shrugged off her words, murmuring, "Well, I couldn't very well have left you like that."

"Someone else did," Devon said under her breath before she could stop herself.

She was referring to the SOB who'd gotten her pregnant and then abandoned her, Cody thought. Ordinarily an easygoing, mild-mannered man, he could feel his temper spiking. Who did that kind of thing?

"About that—" Cody began.

"I don't want to talk about it," Devon responded, her tone shutting down any conversation that might have gone in that direction.

"Then we won't," he told Devon.

But mentally, Cody made a note to look into the matter for his own edification as soon as the dust settled. Someone needed to be taught a lesson about basic responsibility.

Looking back at the entire incident now, Cody was well aware that had he not happened along when he did, Devon could have very well died, either in childbirth or right after that from blood loss. It wasn't something he wanted to think about, but, on the other hand, the man who had gotten Devon pregnant and

then pulled a vanishing act had to be held accountable for this.

Unless she had felt compelled to run away from
him, Cody thought suddenly. But for some reason,
as he reconsidered the matter, he didn't think that
was the case.

Telling himself to revisit the subject later, when he
could do something about it, Cody turned his attention back to the woman in the hospital bed for now.

"Are you thirsty?" he asked her. He could see not
wanting to eat right now—although that had never
been his problem. But she needed to stay hydrated.
"Do you want something to drink?"

The second he asked, Devon became aware of
being thirsty. Very thirsty. She couldn't remember
the inside of her mouth ever feeling as dry as it did
right at this moment.

She nodded. "Some water would be nice," she told
him.

But as he rose to his feet, a sense of panic suddenly
swooped out of nowhere, seizing her. Looking back,
her reaction made Devon feel ashamed of herself, but
at the moment she felt completely overwhelmed by
the feeling. She reached out and grabbed his hand,
trying to hold on to it.

"Don't leave me." It was almost a plea. The ner-
vousness undulating through her took Devon's breath
away.

If her request surprised him, Cody gave no indication. "I'm not going anywhere," he assured Devon.
"There's water right over here." He pointed to the
faucet over the sink. "Just a couple of steps away."

Devon flushed, feeling like a complete idiot. What

the hell was wrong with her? This wasn't like her at all. She wasn't normally needy or clingy. If anything, she prided herself on being the total opposite.

"Sorry," she murmured as she accepted the water-filled paper cup he brought back to her. "Must be all these hormones acting up," she told him. "You can leave if you want to. I'll be fine."

He didn't buy it for a minute. And even if she really wanted him to, he wasn't about to leave her alone. Cody planted himself on the chair that he'd pulled up next to her bed earlier and got as comfortable as he could.

"Don't have anywhere I need to be but here," he replied simply.

"No wife and family waiting for you at home?" she asked. She'd taken up enough of his time. If he had people waiting for him, if wasn't fair of her to make him stay.

"No wife," Cody told her.

"No family?" she pressed, unable to imagine someone like Cody being utterly unattached.

"Oh, I've got family," Cody assured her. "But it's not like we tuck each other into bed."

Half the time Connor did act like their father, but it was Connor who had always said to never leave a job unfinished and, as far as Cody was concerned, seeing to this new mother's needs through the night qualified as a job that he had undertaken.

"Do you have brothers and sisters?" she asked, curious.

It was a question, but he also caught a rather wistful tone in her voice, which in turn had him asking a question of his own.

"Are you an only child?"

Cody could see that Devon was struggling to erect a protective wall around herself or, at the very least, a protective shield. But she wasn't fast enough. He'd glimpsed the vulnerable woman who was just beneath the bravado and the careless act.

Devon frowned, ignoring his question.

"How many brothers and sisters?" she asked, stubbornly pressing on.

Cody felt he had gotten his answer about her family dynamics. "Two of the first, one of the second," he told her.

Devon tried to envision them all around the dining table, talking over one another, arguing, laughing. "Parents?"

Cody shook his head. "Not for a while now," he told her quietly.

So his life wasn't as perfect as she thought. Devon felt sympathy stirring within her. "Me neither."

"Guess that gives us something in common," Cody replied.

Devon nodded. For just a single moment, she felt close to the man who had rescued her. "Guess so," she murmured.

He wanted to keep her talking and thinking of something else. "Were you headed somewhere?" When she didn't answer him, he gently pressed, "When I found you, where were you going?"

A single tear spilled out of the corner of her eye, leaving a trail along her cheek until it stained the sheet beneath her ear.

"Doesn't matter now," she told him quietly.

Jack was gone and he had left intentionally, deserting her as well as the baby she now realized he'd never really wanted. She was not going to lower herself any further by continuing to search for him. Jack wasn't going to take her back and even if he did, she didn't want him to. But it would have been nice to recover her mother's jewelry.

The next moment, she banished the thought. Time to get on with her life. Hers and her daughter's. She just needed to find somewhere to stay until she could figure out what her next move was going to be.

"Is there anyone you want me to call for you?" Cody offered. "Anyone you want to come for you?"

Devon shook her head in response to each question. She had a few girlfriends, but they were more like acquaintances than people she could turn to in a time of need or share anything of importance with. Besides, they were all in another state. She couldn't think of a single person who would go out of their way for her.

"Nobody," she told him stoically.

"No family at all? No friends?" he pressed, doing his best not to sound incredulous. In his experience, everyone had *someone* to turn to. He couldn't begin to imagine how alone she had to feel.

His protective instincts went up several degrees.

"Nobody you need to waste your time or your breath calling," she told him flatly.

He'd taken in enough strays in his time to know one when he saw one. It didn't matter that the former were all animals and she was definitely a flesh-and-blood human being.

The woman was obviously without any binding ties and most definitely on her own.

"And no," she said, her eyes meeting his—hers daring him to display even an ounce of pity, "I have nowhere to go."

"Don't worry about that," he said dismissively. "We've got plenty of room at the ranch. You and Layla can stay there until you can get back on your feet and decide what you want to do."

"You mean stay with you?"

And here she'd thought that he was different. How gullible could she be?

Cody could hear the wariness in her voice. He did what he could to set her mind at ease immediately.

"With my family," he corrected. "Those siblings you asked me about, we all live together on the ranch my father left us. And, if you don't want to stay with us, there's always Miss Joan's." He saw a quizzical look enter Devon's eyes. "She's taken in her share of people who were passing through Forever, on their way to nowhere."

"You mean charity cases," she said indignantly. "I'm not—"

"Nope," he said, cutting in. "She's already been by. Told me to tell you she's got a job waiting for you once you're up to it. She runs the local diner and could always use another waitress." Devon was looking very tired, Cody thought. "Okay, enough talking. Right now," he told her, "your only job is to get stronger."

She started to protest that he had no business telling her what to do or acting as if he was in charge of her life.

She wanted to, but the words didn't come because she had fallen asleep again.

"Attagirl," Cody murmured, drawing the blanket

back up over her, tucking Devon in. He ran the back of his hand along her cheek.

She looked so vulnerable and innocent. Something stirred a little harder within him.

"Get some sleep," he whispered as he planted himself back into the chair.

*Chapter Seven*

Open six days a week, Forever's medical clinic's doors were not officially open this morning until nine o'clock. That didn't mean that neither Alisha or Dan came in at that time. Both doctors, especially Dan, made a point of arriving at least forty-five minutes to an hour earlier.

This morning, because he had a patient who had remained at the clinic overnight, Dan came in a few minutes after seven to see how both she and her impromptu "nurse" were doing.

Dan considered *everyone* in and around Forever as patients he had either previously ministered to or would be ministering to in the near future. The health and welfare of the good citizens of Forever were a perpetual concern for him.

Since arriving in Forever several years ago, Dan hadn't even remotely been tempted to do things in half measures.

Entering the clinic through the back entrance, Dan eased into the single-story building and made his way into the room where he had left Devon recovering from her emergency surgery. The operation, plus the ordeal of childbirth, had taken a heavy toll on

the woman. She was going to need some time to recover even though she struck him as otherwise being
a rather healthy, strong woman.

The doctor found Cody in a chair right beside
the young mother's bed—just as he had expected he
would. Dan made a quick assessment of his patient's
condition. His first overall impression was that Devon
looked a great deal better than she had last night.
There was color—not just a flush but actual, well-
distributed color—back in her cheeks and that was
always a good sign.

At first glance, both his patient and her rough-
around-the-edges guardian angel appeared to be
sound asleep.

But within a few seconds, Dan saw Devon stirring.
And then she opened her eyes.

It never got old, Dan thought, pleased. Although he
had been practicing medicine for a number of years
now, the exhilarating feeling he experienced whenever he witnessed someone getting better because
of his efforts still flashed through him like a bright,
gleaming thunderbolt.

Best adrenaline rush ever, Dan thought as he
smiled at Devon.

"You gave us all quite a scare, young lady," he
told her. His smile widened. "How are you feeling,
Devon? You don't mind if I call you Devon, do you?"

"You're the doctor?" she asked. He was still
dressed in jeans and a bulky sweater, so she wasn't
sure. She'd been unconscious when Cody had brought
her into the clinic.

"One of them," Dan confirmed.

Devon's eyes crinkled as she smiled at him. "Seeing as how I'm told that you saved my life, you can call me anything you want."

"Just part of a team," Dan told her, neatly deflecting the compliment. "If anyone deserves credit for saving your life, it would be Cody over there," he said quietly, nodding in the sleeping deputy's direction. "If he hadn't found you and brought you in when he did, the only thing I would have been able to do for you is call the official time of death. You might want to think about buying a lottery ticket because you really *are* the definition of *lucky*."

The emptiness suddenly and unexpectedly got to her. Cody had said that Layla was spending the night at the doctor's house. Had Cody lied for some reason? Or was her baby not well and had to be rushed to a hospital?

"My baby—" she began.

"—is perfect," Dan told her with a smile. "She spent the night at my home with my wife. She'll be bringing your daughter in shortly. So," he continued in the manner of a doctor who had done this countless times already, "to get back to my question, how are you feeling?"

She didn't even have to stop and think before answering. "Relieved. Tired. Very, very sore," Devon told him, rattling off her answers.

Dan nodded as he calmly took down a blood pressure cuff from a hook on the wall. Wrapping the cuff around Devon's arm that was closest to him, he proceeded to pump it up, then slowly released the air through a valve. He took note of the numbers.

"Sounds wonderfully normal to me," he confirmed. "You took excellent care of yourself during this pregnancy and this is obviously the payoff for all your conscientiousness," Dan acknowledged. Removing the cuff, he folded it and set the machine aside.

"So I'm free to go?" Devon asked. Her tone sounded far more eager than she actually felt.

"I think an extra day in bed would be advised," Dan counseled, writing down the reading that had registered on the blood pressure's monitor.

"Here?" she asked uncertainly.

Dan nodded. "It's a bed and there are four of us here to look in on you. Can't beat that," he told her cheerfully.

Despite the various situations she had found herself in over the course of her young life, the one constant that had never changed was Devon's sense of pride. Poor or not, she had always found a way to pay her way, even though, as a substitute elementary school teacher, she had never been even remotely flush.

"I can't pay you right now," she qualified, letting him know that she did consider it a debt she intended to make good on.

"I'm not really concerned about that right now," Dan informed her. "This isn't exactly a cash-and-carry business, you know."

"But—" she began to protest.

"Devon," he went on firmly, "if I were in this for the money, I would have never left New York."

Surprised, Devon looked at him more closely. "You're from New York?"

He liked the surprise in her voice. It meant that he was finally on his way to shedding the accent that had been such a major factor in his speech pattern.

"Yes."

"Why did you leave?" she asked incredulously. It had to be a complete shock to his system, going from New York City to a town like this.

In his place, she knew she wouldn't have come out. To her, New York represented the very best of the civilized world and being part of that was everything she would have ever aspired to.

"I made a promise," Dan answered vaguely. Never mind that the promise he'd made was to his younger brother, who, at the time he made it, was no longer among the living—something he would feel eternally responsible for.

Before she could ask another question, their conversation—even though they had kept their voices at a low level—succeeded in rousing Cody.

Cody was awake and automatically on his feet in the same instant.

"What's wrong?" he asked, even as his brain struggled to get itself back into gear.

He really didn't remember falling asleep. The last thing Cody could recall was tucking the blanket around Devon again. Turned out that the woman was a fitful sleeper.

"Nothing," Dan answered him, his tone laid-back and easy. "Everything seems right on track with our new mother here. You, however, look like hell," Dan commented, taking a longer, closer look at the younger man.

"Yeah, Connor already mentioned that." Looking past the doctor, he glanced at Devon. He was far more concerned about her condition than he was about his own appearance. "So she's okay?" he pressed, wanting to be reassured. Wanting to leave no margin for doubt.

"Appears that way. Her blood pressure is remarkably low, all things considered. I'm going to have Dr. Cordell-Murphy give her a thorough physical exam later to confirm that." Dan said, "Why don't you go home now and get some sleep?"

"I slept here," Cody answered, dismissing the well-intended suggestion.

"And you look it. These chairs weren't exactly built to give anyone a comfortable night's sleep," Dan pointed out.

Cody shrugged the words away. He was about to say something else in his own defense when they heard the back door being opened.

The next moment, Dan's wife, Tina, walked into the room, a pink bundle in her arms.

The second she saw her baby, Devon immediately began to pull herself up into a sitting position.

"Hold it," Dan cautioned. The doctor pressed a button on an attached keypad and raised the mattress that was beneath her shoulders until he'd achieved an upright position for her.

"That's better," he pronounced.

"Your mama's been waiting for you, precious," Tina Davenport cooed to the baby she was holding. "There you go, say hi to your mama," the doctor's wife instructed, shifting the baby from her own arms into Devon's. "Your daughter has to qualify as one of the sweetest-dispositioned babies I've ever had the fortune of interacting with." As she took a step back from the bed, she added, "I'd say that's a pretty good omen." She told her husband, "See you tonight," and then paused to assure Devon, "You're in very capable hands."

And with that, Tina left the clinic the same way she had entered.

"Okay, she's been fed and changed as of forty minutes ago. Hopefully, the latter will last for a little bit. If she needs changing, use that buzzer," Dan told his patient, indicating the keypad he had previously used to raise the mattress. "Holly or Debi will be in to do the honors for you." His grin was infectious as he went on to tell the brand-new mother, "I'd take advantage of that if I were you."

Turning from Devon, the doctor took another long look at Cody. Except for yesterday, he had never seen the young deputy in anything but top, alert condition. That wasn't the case at the moment.

"Go home, Cody. You really do look like hell."

"That seems to be the popular assessment of the day," Cody murmured. But he had a job to get to and if he was leaving the clinic, he was going to the sheriff's office. He'd already missed too much work. "Okay, since everyone seems to think I'm bringing down the atmosphere, I'll get out of your hair." He asked Dan, "Do you know when you'll be letting her leave?"

"All things being equal, I'll release Devon and her baby tomorrow morning around when we open the clinic." Turning toward his patient, he told Devon in the next breath, "You're quite welcome to stay with my family and me once you're discharged."

"My place is closer," Alisha interjected, coming in and presenting herself to Devon and her baby. "So you might want to come and stay with Brett and me. I have a ground-floor spare bedroom that—"

"Devon already has a place to stay," Cody informed the two doctors, then nodded back toward Devon and the tiny pink bundle in her arms. "She'll be staying at the ranch." Shifting to look at Devon, he promised, "I'll be back."

And with that, Cody left the room.

Nodding at Holly and Debi, who were both already in the reception area, pulling files and bracing themselves for the onslaught of patients, Cody walked out of the building.

Flint was no longer tied to the hitching post. In place of the stallion, his truck was now standing there, apparently ready for travel.

*Connor*, Cody thought gratefully. *Always there to fill in the gaps.*

TRUE TO HIS WORD, Cody went straight to the sheriff's office.

He half expected the office to be empty. Unlike the clinic staff, who were in almost constant demand, Rick and his deputies were considered necessary in terms of generating goodwill within the town and its surrounding area. Their job was not so much focused on keeping the peace—what he'd told Devon was true: the peace more or less kept itself. Their jobs were focused on pitching in to help its residents with whatever they needed.

Occasionally, it was to locate a child who had wandered off. And every so often it was to mediate a dispute between two citizens, both of whom believed they were in the right over, like as not, some trivial matter.

The department got its share of phone calls asking them to find pets that had gone astray or to tackle an aggressive coyote or two that had gotten too brazen for the town's own good.

And, of course, there was Nathan McLane, the de facto town drunk. Nathan was harmless. Long ago he had chosen resting on a stool in Murphy's Saloon over sitting in his living room, listening to his less-than-sympathetic wife recite a list of all his short-comings and outright failures.

On a few occasions, Nathan had actually attempted—never successfully—to walk home from the saloon. Those were times that either Cody, Rick or one of the deputies would bring the man in and lock him up for the night to sleep it off.

Gabe Rodriguez was already at his desk when Cody came in, searching through something on the computer.

"'Morning," Cody murmured as he passed Gabe on his way to the rather ancient-looking coffee maker.

There was a full pot of freshly brewed coffee in the decanter, the enticing aroma filling the air.

"'Morning, stranger," Gabe murmured before looking up.

And then he did.

Gabe had been filled in on yesterday's excitement. News traveled like the proverbial wildfire in a town where sighting the first robin of spring was considered newsworthy.

"Hey, have you been to bed yet?" Gabe asked the

department's newest deputy. "'Cause you really look like he—"

Cody held his hand up to stop the rest of the sentence. "If you say what I think you're going to say, you need to know that I can't be held accountable for my reaction."

Gabe laughed. "I take it that someone else already told you?"

"I don't think there's anyone left in town who *hasn't* told me," Cody commented wearily.

He had to admit that he felt pretty worn-out right about now. Yesterday was finally beginning to catch up to him.

"So, then, why don't you go home and get some rest?" Gabe asked. It struck him as the only logical conclusion.

"Because I was already out yesterday and I don't want to lose my job for taking too much personal time," Cody explained, adding, "I really like this job."

Gabe clearly wasn't following Cody's reasoning. "Why would you lose your job? You were busy saving a tourist's life. That's supposed to be one of the things we get paid for, remember? Saving people. It's not like you took time away from capturing the culprits responsible for some kind of crime spree."

Cody's head was definitely foggy and he wasn't absorbing things as quickly as he normally did.

"Too many words," he muttered, tipping back his coffee mug.

Gabe tried again. "In a nutshell, Rick clocked you in. You were on the job yesterday, protecting and serving, not playing hooky." Getting up, Gabe came over to Cody's desk, where the tired deputy had more or less collapsed into his chair rather than simply sitting down. "That means you're free to go home, Cody."

But Cody shook his head. "I'm waiting to get my second wind. If I lie down now, I probably won't get up until tomorrow morning."

Gabe sighed and turned back to go to his desk. "Suit yourself," he said with a shrug.

*I generally do*, Cody thought with a smile. The tricky part, though, he couldn't help thinking, was getting through today without falling asleep on the job.

The fact that he intended to look in on Devon and the baby at lunchtime and then at the end of the day helped him to rev up his engine.

## Chapter Eight

"How is she?" Sheriff Rick Santiago asked Cody less than half an hour later as he walked into the office.

Cody looked up to find that the sheriff had paused by his desk on his way to the crowded cubbyhole in the rear of the office that served as his work space.

Cody couldn't help thinking of the sick feeling he'd had in the pit of his stomach when he'd first become aware of all the blood that Devon had lost.

"Better than I actually thought she'd be at this point," he confessed. "Turns out that she's pretty resilient and has a great constitution. Doc thinks she'll be strong enough to leave the clinic by tomorrow morning."

Rick nodded, taking in his deputy's words. "Dan thinks a lot of the credit belongs to you," Rick said matter-of-factly. Through the whimsy of fate, Dan Davenport was his brother-in-law, married to Olivia's younger sister, Tina. They'd all had dinner late last night. "Word around Murphy's Saloon has it that you'll be able to amass a lot of free drinks on that particular story," Rick commented.

"I don't really drink," Cody reminded his boss.

"I'm sure the details can be worked out when the

time comes," Rick surmised. He was fairly certain that if he didn't want alcohol, then Cody was going to be in for his share of hot meals at Miss Joan's. "I really didn't expect to see you in today."

"Planning on giving away my job already?" Cody asked dryly.

"Nobody I know would be a good candidate for it. Takes a certain talent to be able to mix boredom with getting things done. Right now, there're no takers."

"I tried to tell him to go home, Sheriff," Gabe told Rick, speaking up.

"The McCulloughs have always been a stubborn bunch," Rick reminded his other deputy. He turned toward Cody. "You find out what her story is yet?" he asked.

"Story?" Cody repeated. His brain felt as if it was wrapped in a thin layer of cotton. Maybe he should have gone home to grab a quick nap, he thought, beginning to reconsider his position.

The sheriff nodded. "What was she doing out there by herself in her condition?"

He had a feeling that Devon felt that she'd had no choice in the matter.

"She didn't give me any details and when I asked her, she really didn't want to talk about it," Cody told the sheriff. "I thought I'd give her a few days to get better before I start to ask her any questions, if it's all right with you."

"No problem," Rick agreed. "It can wait. Got a place for her to stay yet?"

There was probably no shortage of doors that would be opened to the young mother. If nothing else, the good people of Forever were generous to a fault.

"Several places," Cody said, not wanting to get into the fact that it didn't matter who else volunteered to take Devon and her baby in. At the end of the day, he was still taking the two of them to the ranch. The way he saw it, she was his responsibility until such time that she was able to leave on her own power.

"Do we know who she is?" Rick asked.

"Her name is Devon Bennett," Joe Lone Wolf said as he walked in. The sheriff's brother-in-law was carrying a box of pastries that he proceeded to deposit on the center table.

Rick gave the box and its contents a quick once-over. "What's the occasion?" Rick asked.

"I stopped at the diner to get some coffee—no offense but ours hasn't been good since Alma retired," he complained, referring to Gabe's sister, who had brought him into the department before she married Miss Joan's step-grandson, "and Miss Joan said to bring these to 'the hero.' I figured that meant you," Joe said, looking at Cody.

Cody shook his head, disavowing any connection to the title. "I'm not a hero," he protested.

"I figure the young woman might have a different opinion about that," Rick commented, selecting a cream-filled pastry from the top. He took a bite before heading to his office. "Damn but that's good. That's got to be Angel's handiwork," he said to Gabe. "You are one lucky son of a gun, Deputy. It's a mystery to me why you haven't blown up to at least twice your normal size since you married that woman."

Picking out a pastry for himself, Gabe sat down at his desk. "It's not like that. Angel cooks and bakes all day long at the diner. The last thing she wants to do when she comes home is cook."

There was genuine pity in Rick's eyes as he looked at his deputy. "You mean you're not going home every night to fantastic meals?"

"I wouldn't say that," Gabe corrected and told the sheriff, "I make most of our meals."

Cody laughed for the first time that morning. "So then I take it you're living on sandwiches? No wonder you're not fat—don't forget, I've had some of your cooking," he reminded his friend.

Gabe drew himself up to his full height. "I'll have you know that I'm a damn good cook," he informed the man he'd known since childhood.

"You just keep on telling yourself that, Gabe," Cody said as he got back to the search he'd started to conduct on his computer.

It was, Rick thought with a hint of a smile as he finally walked back to his small office, business as usual.

Couldn't ask for better than that.

THE FOLLOWING MORNING, Cody popped into the sheriff's office to let him know that he was going to be picking up Devon and the baby at the clinic.

"Take all the time you need," Rick told him. "Nothing of consequence is going on here."

Cody lost no time in getting over to the clinic.

Over the course of the day before, he'd been out on patrol twice, walking the streets of Forever, and maybe it was just his imagination, but he could have sworn that people were smiling at him more broadly than usual.

Cody knew he should just enjoy it and ride the wave of warm approval, but he was a man who felt more comfortable fading into the shadows than being thrust out onto center stage.

Still, as he made his way to the clinic this morning, there were people out who were more than willing to call out their approval.

"Way to go, Deputy."

"Nice job, Cody."

"You did your daddy proud."

The last one, coming from one of his father's oldest friends, tugged at his heart, even though he did his best not to show how affected he was by it.

Cody nodded in response to each and every acknowledgment, trying to be polite while still remaining as self-effacing as usual.

Making his way to the back of the clinic, he saw that the door to the room where Devon was was partially closed.

He would have knocked on the door if he hadn't heard the buzz of mingling voices. He paused for a moment, thinking that perhaps one of the two doctors was in the room with Devon. He definitely didn't want to intrude, especially if she happened to be getting an exam.

"You don't have to stand on ceremony."

The deep male voice was coming from behind him.

Cody turned around just in time to see Dan.

"Go on in," Dan urged, waving him into the room ahead of him. "I'm giving her a clean bill of health," he told Cody.

Opening the door, Cody saw that not only wasn't Devon alone, several women were in the room with her. In addition to Devon, Holly, Miss Joan and his sister, Cassidy, were all gathered around the hospital bed, leaving precious little space in the room.

They all seemed to be talking at once.

Cody wasn't surprised to see Miss Joan—the people in town had long since given up attempting to pigeonhole the older woman. She was the source of never-ending surprises. Miss Joan showed up wherever she damn well pleased, whenever she felt she was needed. It was obvious by the tray on the side counter that Miss Joan had brought in breakfast for Devon.

And Holly was the nurse, so of course she had every reason to be at a patient's bedside.

It was Cassidy's presence here in Devon's room that threw him.

Beating around the bush had always struck him as a waste of time. He got right to the heart of the matter.

"What are you doing here?" he asked his sister.

Rather than answer him immediately, Cassidy tossed her long blond hair over her shoulder, narrowed her blue eyes and gave him a long, thoughtful once-over.

"Since when have you been put in charge of where I go and what I do?" she asked. Before Cody could comment on his sister's unofficial challenge, Cassidy told him, "If you must know, I'm convincing Devon here that you're harmless." Taking him aside for a second, she added in a lower voice, "I also brought her some clothes I thought she might find handy."

It was Cassidy's tactful way of not mentioning the fact that he'd told her that Devon only had the clothes on her back—and those had been cut off her when he'd brought her in to stop the hemorrhaging.

The *harmless* remark Cassidy had made had caught his attention. Cody looked quizzically from his sister to the woman he had come to take back to the family ranch.

"Come again?"

"I'm vouching for you, Cody," Cassidy said cheerfully. "For all of us at the ranch, really. You do have a shifty face," she patted his cheek by way of underscoring her statement. "Can't blame the poor woman for holding your invitation to come stay at the ranch suspect." Cassidy shrugged carelessly. "I thought that if she knew that you weren't offering to take her to some den of iniquity, she'd relax and agree to stay there while she recuperated."

Flashing a smile at the woman in the bed, Cassidy went on to tell her brother. "It's all settled. She's going to be coming with us."

Despite the fact that she liked the idea of being with Cody and his siblings, Devon felt compelled to offer at least some sort of token protest.

"Layla and I could always stay at the hotel," she told Cody. "Holly said that the one in town is only about three years old."

"And just what would you be using for money, my dear?" Miss Joan asked bluntly. "You said that no-good SOB took your joint savings when he skipped out on you."

Cody shook his head. Leave it to Miss Joan to find out more about Devon in the space of a few minutes than he had in all the hours he'd sat by her bedside the other night, keeping vigil.

Devon attempted to brazen her way through it. "I

was thinking of offering to work my debt off once I was on my feet."

"Very noble of you," Miss Joan commented. "Also pointless since you have all these people here offering to take you in, including me. Hospitality beats servitude seven days a week and twice on Sunday," the older woman pointed out.

Feeling outnumbered and outtalked, Cody glanced at the only other male in the room.

As if reading his mind, Dan said, "Dr. Cordell-Murphy gave her a physical yesterday." He smiled at Devon. "Mama and her baby are free to leave the clinic whenever she's ready." Looking at his patient, he added. "You're also free to spend another night here if you'd feel better doing that. You know, one more night to build up your strength."

Devon flashed the doctor a grateful smile. "No disrespect intended, Doctor, but if it's all the same to you, I'd rather get out of your way and settle in somewhere else."

"No disrespect taken," Dan assured her. "So, where'll it be? Miss Joan's home, the McCullough ranch or Holly's house?"

She appreciated the overwhelming generosity of the people in the room. Even so, she wished she had the option of politely turning down all three offers and getting on with her life on her own.

But it wasn't just her life that she was accountable for. She didn't have the luxury of pride where her daughter's comfort was at stake.

"The ranch," Devon finally said quietly. "But I want you to understand that I intend to pay you back," she insisted.

"There's nothing to pay back," Cody replied.

"It's not like Connor has a rental rate posted for the extra bedrooms," Cassidy told the other woman. "Just having that little darling around—" she nodded at the infant lying in the cradle that had been donated to the clinic "—will be payment enough for Connor, trust me." Cassidy gave Devon an encouraging smile. "For all of us, really. The two of you will brighten up the house," Cassidy assured her.

"I guess it's settled, then," Devon said, praying she was making the right decision and that she wouldn't regret it.

But if she was being honest with herself, she really had no other options open to her at this point.

"Good," Cassidy pronounced. "By the way, I brought you a change of clothes, just in case you don't have anything serviceable to wear."

Devon exchanged looks with Cody's sister. "You heard," she guessed. Word apparently got around very fast. She'd been in town only a little more than forty-eight hours.

"That that bastard made off with your clothes when he left?" Cassidy wasn't really asking a question. "Yes, I heard."

"You're better off without that lowlife," Miss Joan declared firmly. "You ask me, losing a few articles of clothing is well worth the price," she told Devon, patting the younger woman's hand. Miss Joan was the heart of the town, but she came with a crusty shell— except when it came to children. The transformation was enough to render a person speechless. "And when you're feeling up to it, I plan to hold a baby shower for you at the diner."

Devon looked at the woman, clearly confused again. "Baby showers are held before the baby's born," she pointed out, skipping over the part that was glaringly obvious to her. Baby showers were thrown by family and friends. These people were neither to her. In her opinion, they had already gone over and above the call of duty helping her.

Since her mother had died, Devon had come to expect nothing from people. That way she found that she was never disappointed.

"At my age, I've learned not to let a few silly rules get in my way or stop me," Miss Joan was saying to her. "And in my opinion, this little lady is definitely in need of a shower."

She had already assessed that the young mother had absolutely nothing when it came to the various items that a newborn required.

"Why don't we clear out and let Devon get dressed?" Holly suggested tactfully. Turning toward the young mother, she made her an offer. "I can stick around if you need any help putting on your new clothes."

"And that'll give me a few more minutes to hold this little darling in my arms," Miss Joan said, cooing to the baby she held close as she walked out of the room.

Miss Joan was followed out by Cody and Cassidy, as well as the doctor.

"Well, I've got a backlog of patients still waiting for me," Dan said by way of parting. He looked over his shoulder back into the room. "Call me if you need me," he told Devon.

Miss Joan waited until the doctor had disappeared

into an exam room. "Did you happen to catch sight of the scum who robbed her blind and then cut out on that poor girl?"

"He probably took off in another direction," Cody guessed. He didn't add that he intended to check any reports of recently stolen vehicles within a thirty-mile radius. Layla's father would have needed some mode of transportation since there was no other way to get around.

After he found the man—and he had little doubt that he would—he wasn't sure exactly what he would do. But that wasn't something he had to work out yet. First, he had to catch the bastard. The rest would follow.

## Chapter Nine

"*That's* your house?" Devon asked Cody in unabashed wonder.

She was sitting in the rear of the truck just behind the passenger seat. Layla's car seat—Tina Davenport had insisted on lending it—was next to her, strapped in right behind the driver's seat.

Devon's question referred to the building she was looking at, a warm, rambling, three-storied structure that seemed to grow larger and more overwhelming the closer the truck came to it.

Cody nodded. "Well, mine and my family's," he told her.

A sliver of wistful envy stirred through her. For Devon, home had been a series of one-bedroom apartments, studio apartments and, on the occasions when her mother couldn't find any work, the backseat of a second-hand SUV or a truck.

"How do you keep from getting lost in it?" Devon asked.

"You get used to it," Cody assured her. "Besides, it's not as big on the inside as it looks."

"It couldn't be," she murmured under her breath, awestruck. And then a practical question occurred to her, one that she hadn't even considered earlier when Cody had convinced her to stay at his place. "Are your brothers okay with my staying here? I know that it's all right with your sister, but a lot of men don't like having their space invaded," she pointed out.

She certainly didn't want to repay Cody for coming to her rescue by causing his brothers to give him grief.

"Well, as you already noticed, this is a large house," Cody told her. "You're not exactly going to be in anyone's way unless they come looking for you."

Cody pulled up the truck in front of the main house. Devon still felt rather uncertain about staying here, but it was too late to change her mind. By the time she had unbuckled her seat belt, Cody had already rounded the truck's hood and was on the passenger side, ready to assist her in any way that she needed him to.

The front door opened even as Cody was pulling open the passenger door on the truck.

Devon saw what appeared to be a slightly older version of Cody run down the three steps that led from the porch.

"Hi," he said, flashing what looked like an identical smile at her. "Welcome to the house. I'm Cole."

"Hi, Cole," she said, returning his greeting. "I'm… dizzy. Wow."

Devon blew out a breath, suddenly feeling a wave of weakness washing over her. It took her completely by surprise because, over the course of the day, she'd felt she was getting stronger. In her opinion, this was a definite setback.

It occurred just as she was stepping out of the vehicle on the passenger side. The second her foot touched the ground, her leg buckled right from under her, sending her straight into Cody's arms. Luckily he'd had the presence of mind to position himself right in front of her, just in case.

Devon flushed, embarrassed. She wasn't supposed to feel like a limp rag doll. "I'm sorry," she said.

"For what? Being human? Not necessary," Cody told her. He was holding her to him and did his best to search her face from that angle. "Do you want to go back to the clinic?"

"Oh Lord, no," Devon cried emphatically. "Not that everyone wasn't nice to me there—they were." Especially when she considered the fact that she had no ties to the town or anyone there. "But I've got to keep moving forward."

"Well, for now, we're putting that 'moving forward' exercise on hold." The next second, rather than putting her back into the truck, he easily lifted her in his arms. "If you don't want to go back to the clinic, okay, but you're going straight to bed,"

She couldn't put him out like this, nor could she allow herself to depend on him. The man was no one to her and owed her nothing. In contrast, she and Jack had planned forever together and that hadn't stopped him from leaving.

"Put me down. I can take care of myself," she protested with feeling.

"That's debatable," Cody answered, making no effort to set her down.

Devon tried again. "My baby," she protested, reaching out to the infant still in the backseat.

"Got her covered. Cole," he called out to his brother, "bring the baby."

For his part, Cole looked a little perplexed. "How do I get her out of this contraption?" he asked, referring to the car seat.

"Bring the whole thing," Cody said. "Just open up the straps tethering the car seat to the truck," he told his older brother.

"If you say so," Cole murmured, trying to get the seat loose.

Cody debated taking Devon inside and putting her in the guest bedroom before coming back out to lend Cole a hand. That would have been the simplest way to go, but he sensed that it would also cause Devon more than a little stress and concern.

"I'm going to set you down for a minute," he told Devon, returning her to her seat. "Okay?"

The world insisted on spinning, even though she was doing her very best to focus on keeping it still.

"Do what you have to do to get her untangled," Devon urged, trying not to let Cody see just how weak she suddenly felt. The last thing she wanted was to divert his attention away from Layla.

Despite Cole's consternation, it took very little effort to untangle the straps that had constrained Layla's car seat.

"*Now* you can take her into the guest bedroom," Cody told his brother, turning his attention back to Devon.

This time, she allowed Cody to pick her up without complaint. She had to admit that having his strong arms around her made her feel safe.

The next moment, she was silently upbraiding herself for feeling that way.

*Safe?*

*What's wrong with you? When are you going to learn? No one is going to be your crutch. You're the only one you can depend on, not some good-looking, sexy deputy sheriff.*

She was doing her very best to rein in her feelings while also holding them at arm's length, but she was failing at both. There was this hunger within her to allow someone in, someone who would help her banish the incredible loneliness that had hollowed out her insides.

Cody was aware of her tightening her arms around his neck. Despite the warm feeling being generated within him, he told himself that she was doing it just because she was afraid of being dropped.

*Don't make anything of this that it isn't*, he warned himself.

"Not too much longer," he promised out loud.

Devon didn't loosen her hold.

Cody carried her into the house and then made a sharp turn to his left. There was a bedroom just off the main living area, its window looking out on what amounted to the front yard.

"This is your room for now," Cody told her, then quickly corrected himself. "I mean it's your room for however long you need it." He didn't want her to feel as if her presence here created any sort of an inconvenience for him or his family.

"Why?" she asked him unexpectedly as he deposited her on the bed.

He wasn't sure what Devon was asking him. "Why what?"

Just then, Cole came in with the baby. He set the car seat on the floor right next to the bed, then backed off, getting the impression that his older brother wanted to have a few words in private with the woman he had brought to the ranch.

"Why are you doing all this? Why are you taking me in, giving me a place to stay without any strings or deadlines attached?"

He didn't see what the big deal was. In his world, you helped people out, no questions asked. "Because you look like you need it," he told her simply.

"And that's it?"

He looked at her, seeing the suspicious expression in her eyes. Again he caught himself wishing he could get his hands on the man who had run out on her, who had stolen her sense of well-being, not to mention her possessions.

"What more should there be?" he asked her.

"Well, for starters," she said, pointing out the obvious, "I'm nobody to you."

"I wouldn't go that far," he told her. "I mean, I did deliver your baby."

She still couldn't really make any sense out of his behavior. She and Jack had made plans, shared dreams—or so she had thought—and none of that had stopped him from ultimately running out on her.

Not just running out, but taking all her money with him, leaving her stranded and on her own without so much as a backward glance or a note of apology. He hadn't even wasted crocodile tears on her and here was this stranger, someone she hadn't even known three days ago, taking her in and behaving as if he was her newly appointed guardian angel.

"I know," she said to Cody. "But that doesn't obligate you to stick by me."

In a way, she reminded him of Flint. When he'd first come across the stallion, the colt had been extremely skittish and it had taken him a great deal of patience to get Flint to trust him.

He viewed Devon the same way.

"I'd say that we've got a difference of opinion there," he told her mildly. "Now, why don't you get some rest?" he suggested. "Cassidy and Cole will look in on you periodically, make sure that everything's okay."

"Where will you be?" That didn't come out right, Devon realized. She didn't want Cody thinking that she was being clingy because she wasn't. She was just trying to get her bearings and the lay of the land. "I mean—"

"I know what you mean," he told her gently. "I've got to get back to work before they figure out how dispensable I actually am."

Before he could say anything, Cassidy walked in, carrying what appeared to be a drawer. "Where do you want this?" she asked.

"Put it over there." He pointed to the side of the bed. "That way," he added, addressing Devon, "it'll be within reach, but still give you plenty of space to get up."

"What are you doing?" Devon asked, watching him as he arranged the drawer. From her vantage point, she could see that the drawer wasn't empty as she had assumed. It was lined with what appeared to be two blankets, one on top of another.

"Well, it's been a long time since there were any babies in this house, so there are no cribs stored in the attic. But Layla has to sleep somewhere, so until we can get a crib for her, this is going to have to do."

"A bureau drawer?" she questioned incredulously.

"Sure. As long as no one decides to close it, it should be just what she needs." Taking the remaining safety belts off the infant, he lifted her out of the car seat and placed her inside the drawer. "Perfect," he declared.

Even as he made the pronouncement, he saw the infant's eyes flutter shut. "I guess she thinks so, too, because she's falling asleep. I suggest that you do the same," he told Devon.

He started to leave the room when she called him back. "Cody?"

Cody retraced the few steps back to her bed. Devon raised herself up as far as she could and then beckoned him in a little closer. When he bent down, expecting her to share some whispered secret with him, he was surprised to feel the fleeting pass of her lips against his cheek.

He could have sworn he felt a glow spreading out through him in its wake.

Moving back a little, Cody looked at the woman in confusion.

"Thank you," she whispered, her voice brimming with emotion.

And then, the next moment, before he could tell her that she had nothing to thank him for, he saw that Devon had fallen asleep, just like her daughter.

Cody lingered there for a moment, just watching her sleep.

"Don't worry," he whispered to the sleeping pair, "I'll take care of you."

He felt the lighter-than-air imprint of Devon's lips on his skin throughout the drive back to the sheriff's office.

"FEELING BETTER?" CODY ASKED. His shift over, he'd lost no time in hurrying back to the ranch.

Once there, his first order of business was to look in on Devon. There'd been no phone call from either Cassidy or Cole, so he could only assume that everything was going along peacefully.

Devon was up, out of bed and sitting in the rocking chair where Cody's mother had once sat, rocking each one of them to sleep when they were infants. Layla was in her arms. It struck Cody that, somehow, things seemed to have come full circle.

"Yes, much," she answered with a welcoming smile. "Looks like a little angel, doesn't she?" she whispered, still very much in awe that she had given birth to this miracle.

He came around to her side and peered at the tiny, sleeping face.

"She looks like her mother," he told Devon.

The comparison surprised her. "You really think so?"

There was no question about it in Cody's mind. "I do."

Devon looked down at the baby in her arms and then shook her head. "I don't see it," she confessed.

If anything, she thought she could see traces of

Jack in the baby and that bothered her a little. She didn't want to be reminded of all the heartache and humiliation that were involved with Jack's memory.

"Well, she does," Cody said simply. "Have you had anything to eat?" he asked.

"Cassidy brought me something earlier, but I don't have much of an appetite," Devon confessed.

"You need to force yourself," he told her. "You're still eating for two, you know. You've got to build up your strength. You don't want to be bedridden forever."

"I'm not going to be bedridden forever," she protested.

"Good." Opening the bag he'd brought with him, he set out a covered dish on the makeshift tray Cassidy had dug up for her. "This is for you."

Devon raised an eyebrow at the sight of the foil-covered offering.

"Miss Joan had Angel prepare this for you," Cody told her. "She told me that if I didn't make you eat this, she was going to hunt me down and find a way to make me pay for it."

"No, she didn't." Devon dismissed the threat with a laugh.

"Oh yes, she did," he told her in no uncertain terms. "Miss Joan doesn't accept any excuses. She expects results. In your case, that result is in the form of fattening you up."

Cody sat down beside the tray. She allowed him to remove the foil. She had to admit that the scent of the tri-tip sirloin had her mouth watering, which surprised her. She was at the point where she'd assumed no meal would be appealing to her.

Devon had to ask. "Why would she or you care if I eat or not?"

"Why's the sky blue?"

Devon wasn't sure she had heard him correctly. "What?"

"The point is," he clarified, "some things just are—we don't waste time questioning them. Now, start eating so I don't have to try to lie to Miss Joan tomorrow."

"Try to lie?" she repeated. "I'd imagine you're probably very good at it."

He didn't rise to the bait. "Well, I don't lie," he told her simply. "And even if I did, I'd never attempt to lie to Miss Joan. The woman is a human lie detector machine."

"Okay, now I know you're kidding."

"Nope," Cody deadpanned. "That woman has a way of looking at you that makes even a hardened criminal start to confess to things."

Devon was fairly certain he was putting her on, but the sandwich Miss Joan had sent her was far too delicious for her to reject—so she didn't even try.

## Chapter Ten

The scent of fresh brewing coffee had the allure of a siren's song for Cody as he came down the stairs the following morning.

As a rule, Cody, his brothers and sister took turns making breakfast for the others, although between oversleeping and running late, that breakfast more often than not consisted of something simple and basic, like orange juice and dry cereal.

This morning, if he recalled correctly, it was Connor's turn to prepare breakfast. Connor, he knew, favored oatmeal, something the rest of them preferred to pass on.

"Guess you decided to go all out this morning, Connor," Cody commented as he walked into the kitchen.

He stopped dead when he saw that Conner was sitting at the table instead of standing at the stove, preparing four breakfasts. Layla was in her car seat on the table right in front of him, occupying all of his attention.

"Not me," Connor replied, nodding his head at their houseguest.

Devon was standing in front of the stove, her hair

clipped back, and it was her, not Connor, who was busy preparing breakfast for the family. She looked like a vision, Cody couldn't help thinking.

"What's going on?" Cody asked his older brother.

"Hey, don't look at me," Connor protested. He was gently rocking the baby's car seat. "When I came in, Devon was already busy getting breakfast ready. Wait until you try her coffee," he told his brother. It was obvious that the brew had gotten his vote.

"And you let her?" Cody questioned. That wasn't like Connor. His brother normally liked being in control of every situation.

Connor exchanged glances with Devon before answering his brother, "Hey, I learned a long time ago not to get in between a woman and her spatula."

Trying not to look annoyed, Cody crossed over to Devon. "You are supposed to be in bed," he told her sternly.

Devon gave him a wide smile as she kept an eye on two frying pans at the same time. "I'm feeling much better now."

Frustrated, Cody looked at the woman. He couldn't order her around, but he really wished she'd listen to reason. He doubted if she understood how close she had come to dying.

"Just what do you think you're doing?" Cody demanded helplessly.

She spared him another quick glance. "Paying you back in some small way," she told him. "Really, I'm much better," she said, and then, because he didn't look convinced, she added another emphatic "really."

Cody blew out a breath. Talk about being stubborn. "You know, there's no need for you to do this," he insisted.

"Yes, there is," she countered. "I told you yesterday, I am not a charity case."

"Nobody here thinks of you as a charity case," Cody assured her. "Tell her, Connor," he said, enlisting his older brother's help.

"Nobody here thinks of you as a charity case," Connor parroted.

"Then don't make me feel like one." Devon's words were directed at Cody.

After sliding what amounted to a giant omelet onto a plate, Devon cut it into four sections and a sliver. She distributed them onto five plates and added several strips of bacon from the other frying pan to each one.

"Let me do this," she requested as she placed a plate before him and then one in front of Connor. "I promise I won't poison you."

Cody had to admit that the omelet not only looked tempting, but smelled it, as well. He gave up trying to resist.

"I'm not worried about that. If we can survive Connor's cooking, we can survive anything you come up with," he told her. "And if this tastes even half as good as it smells, you will have turned us all into true believers."

"Hey, what is that great smell?" Cole asked, coming into the kitchen. "Did Connor suddenly get some cooking lessons?"

Connor looked up from his plate. "What's wrong with my cooking?" he asked.

Devon had met Connor only fleetingly yesterday

when Cody had brought her to the house. She didn't want the man to think she was trying to upstage him. After all, Connor was head of the household, even though, according to Cody, the house actually belonged to all four of them and they shared equally in all the duties that were involved in running it.

"There's nothing wrong with it. Dinner was wonderful," Devon told the oldest McCullough. "I just thought you and the others might want a reprieve from kitchen duty."

"Amen to that," Connor agreed. "And for the record, Cassidy made dinner last night, not me." In between healthy forkfuls of his serving of Spanish omelet, he told her, "Well, I have to admit, this tastes even better than it smells."

Devon smiled broadly, relieved. She knew that the breakfast she'd prepared was good, but some people might still have taken offense. She was relieved that Connor was not small-minded.

"Hey, what's going on?" Cassidy asked, straggling into the kitchen and joining her brothers. "You guys are making enough noise to wake the dead."

"The hungry dead," Cole interjected, taking in another forkful of his omelet.

Smiling at Devon, Cassidy took a seat. "Well, this is different," she commented as she took her usual seat at the table and pulled over one of the last two plates that Devon had prepared. "Are you getting creative in your old age, Con?"

"Connor can't take the credit for this," Cody told her. "Devon made breakfast today."

"Devon?" Cassidy echoed, looking around the

table at her brothers. "Why are you putting the poor woman to work?"

"Hey, I had nothing to do with it," Cody protested, raising his hands to ward off Cassidy's words of accusation. "When I came into the kitchen, she was already cooking."

"Did she make the coffee, too?" Cole asked. He was nursing a mug that was twice as large as a regular cup.

"Yes, *she* did," Devon answered, wondering if hers didn't measure up to what they were accustomed to.

Cole grinned at her. "Well, I don't know about the others, but as far as I'm concerned, you can stay here forever. Hate to tell you, Connor, but this is a *lot* better than what you come up with. What did you do to this?" he asked after taking another long swallow. "This tastes great." He got up and helped himself to another mugful.

"I used chicory to cut the bitterness," she confessed. It was something her grandmother had taught her, years ago.

"We have that?" Cassidy questioned.

"I found some in the back of your pantry," Devon told her. She'd come across it while rummaging around to see what she could add to the omelet.

"Pure heaven," Cassidy pronounced after draining her cup. "Well, you've got my vote," she told their houseguest cheerfully. "Connor's coffee tastes more like semisoft mud."

Connor leveled a seemingly reproving look at his sister. "You never complained before."

"That's because if I did, you would have stuck me with permanent KP duty." Her eyes shifted to Devon, who had taken a seat beside Cody. She smiled at the other woman. "But now we've got an alternative."

"Hey, Devon's not here to cook for us," Cody said defensively.

Devon put her hand on his to stop him from making any further protests. "It's okay. I need to feel useful," she told him and the others.

"Like Cole said, you've got a place here for as long as you like," Connor told her.

Devon smiled her thanks. She knew that Connor and the others were most likely just being polite, but it was nice to hear and she did like to feel as if she was pulling her own weight. Their approval, well-deserved or not, felt good. It made her realize how much she'd missed hearing that.

Jack never had any actually kind words for her. He'd once told her that if he didn't like something, *then* she'd know about it. To him, the absence of criticism was supposed to be taken as an unspoken compliment. She could never make him understand that she needed more than that, that she needed to actually *hear* praise once in a while. Heaven knew she'd been more than generous and loving when it came to flattering him. But the lesson never seemed to take root with him.

As if feeling left out of the adult conversation, Layla began to stir and within a few seconds, she was mewling.

"Sorry," Cole apologized to her. "I guess we got a little too loud."

Devon was quick to absolve him of any guilt. "No, I think she just got jealous, watching everyone eating breakfast except her," Devon said. Putting everything else on temporary hold, she extracted the infant from her car seat. "She wants some of her own. Let's go, little one," she murmured lovingly to her daughter. "Time to get you fed."

As she began to make her way out of the room, Devon paused to look over her shoulder. "Leave everything the way it is. I'll clean up after Layla's been fed."

"Did you find out anything about her yet?" Connor asked Cody once Devon had retreated to the guest room with Layla.

"No, not yet." He didn't add that he felt it best not to prod Devon for any information. Instead, he wanted to present himself as a willing listener if she decided that she wanted someone to confide in. "Some people take longer to open up than Cassidy," Cody added.

"Hey, I resent that," Cassidy pretended to pout. "Just because I'm friendly—"

"That's one word for it, little sister," Cody countered.

Cassidy raised an eyebrow. "Oh? And what's another word for it?"

"Okay, you two, time-out," Connor told them as he stood up. "Well, I've got a ranch to run so I'd better get to it." His eyes swept over his siblings before he left the table and walked out. "I suggest you do the same. Good meal," he murmured before he disappeared.

"Love to linger over this coffee," Cole told Cody, "but I promised Jackson White Eagle I'd be back to lend a hand at The Healing Ranch," he said, referring to the ranch that had recently had an influx of twice the applicants they normally received. Ever since an article in a national magazine had appeared, citing the ranch's success rate in turning troubled youths around, there had been no shortage of requests for a spot in the innovative program.

"Gotta run, too," Cassidy announced, making a hasty retreat before Cody could ask her any questions.

"Looks like it's just you and me," Cody murmured to the collection of dirty dishes around him at the table. He'd already told the sheriff that he would be coming in later than usual and had gotten the man's blessing.

Despite what Devon had said about leaving everything just as it was, Cody made short work of cleaning up. The dishes were washed, dried and put away. It went faster than he'd thought it would.

He knew he should get going, but he didn't want to just leave without letting Devon know that she would be alone in the house. He wanted to give her a phone number so she could reach him just in case.

Making his way to her room, Cody knocked on Devon's door.

She responded immediately. "Yes?"

Taking that to be an invitation, Cody opened the door. The next second, he stopped dead, stunned and freezing in place.

Devon was sitting on her bed, Layla gathered against her breast. She was still nursing her daughter.

It was—he later thought, looking back—probably the most beautiful sight he had ever seen. But he certainly wasn't free to give voice to that feeling. At the very least, he didn't want to embarrass her.

So he swung his head in the opposite direction, looking away.

"I'm sorry," he told her with feeling. "I didn't mean to just walk in like that. I thought you'd put her down for a nap. I mean—" He fumbled, not knowing what to say to convey just *how* sorry he was for intruding on her in such a private moment.

"It's okay," Devon assured him, her tone understanding as she absolved him of any perceived wrongdoing. "Seems that this little lady is an extremely slow eater."

Deftly pulling her blouse back into place, she put the baby up against her shoulder and began to pat Layla gently on the back.

"Did you want to tell me something?" Devon asked, taking the focus off herself and what Cody had just seen. Theirs, after all, was a rather unique relationship. Cody had already seen far more of her than any other man except for Jack.

Cody was exceedingly grateful to Devon for not making a big deal out of what happened, but by the same token, *because* she was being so nice about it, he felt guilty that it had happened in the first place.

Clearing his throat, he grasped at the excuse she had handed him. "I wanted to know if you needed anything before I went to work."

"You're leaving?" she asked, mildly surprised.

Cody sensed what wasn't being said. "I can stay if you'd rather have someone here."

Devon shook her head. She didn't mean to make him feel that he had to stay with her. Thinking about it, she could use a little alone time herself.

"You've already done a lot for me. I'm not going

to make you stay and hold my hand," she told him. "Layla and I will be fine, won't we, little one?" she said, addressing her question to the infant who was curled up against her shoulder.

Cody took out one of the business cards Cassidy had made up for him as a gift when he'd joined the sheriff's department. It was meant to show Cody how proud they all were of him.

He handed the card to Devon. "That's the phone number at the sheriff's office. Call me if you need anything—or," he added as an afterthought, "if you just want to talk."

She looked at the card before she tucked it into her pocket. "To be honest, what I need right now is some time alone to just pull myself together."

"You look pretty put together to me already." The comment came out before he could censor it. What was wrong with him? He usually exercised more control over himself than this. "Okay, then," he told her as if he hadn't made the other comment, "Connor should be back sometime around noon or so."

"Okay, anything else I should know?" she asked.

He felt she needed to know how much they appreciated what she'd gone out of her way to do, despite what she'd been through herself. "Only that everyone walked out of here smiling because that had to be the best breakfast we've had in a really long time."

Devon couldn't help beaming, even as she dismissed his compliment. "Then I'd say that you and your family are very easily pleased."

"Not really," he interjected, and then told her, "The phone's in the kitchen if you need to call."

Devon nodded, suppressing an amused smile. "I noticed this morning," she replied.

"Right, of course you did." She had to think he was some kind of country bumpkin, Cody upbraided himself.

"You want me to bring you back anything?" he asked just as he was about to leave her bedroom.

"No, I'm good," she assured him. "But be sure to thank Miss Joan for me for the sandwich."

He'd forgotten about that. That Devon had remembered gave him a good feeling about the young woman. She obviously didn't take anything for granted.

"She'll appreciate that," he told her.

He was lingering again, Devon noted. And, as much as she found that she liked having him around, she couldn't allow herself to get used to it or feeling that way.

"You should go," she prompted. "You don't want to be late, especially not on my account."

"Okay, then—you're sure you'll be all right?" he asked one last time.

She rose from the bed and crossed to where he was standing. "I've been on my own for a long time now, Cody. I'll be fine," she assured him.

Then, as if to end the discussion and put an end to any lingering concern he might be harboring, she placed one hand on his shoulder to anchor herself and then rose on her toes. The next moment, she brushed her lips against his cheek.

"Now go," she instructed.

Cody backed out of the room until he felt the heel

of his boot hit the threshold. Only then did he turn around and leave.

He caught himself wanting to remain, just in case, but he knew she was right. He needed to get to work and she probably needed her space right now, just like she had said. He didn't doubt that she needed to sort out her feelings and emotions, not to mention find a way to adjust to being a first-time young mother, something that was bound to throw her world into a tailspin.

As for him, he needed to get to the sheriff's office not just because it was his job, but because he wanted to use the search engines available to him there to see if he could somehow track down the man who had run out on Devon. He wanted the man to own up to his responsibilities. He'd stolen her money and at the very least he needed to make some sort of restitution for that.

If Cody could possibly help it, he wasn't about to let that rotten SOB get away with it.

## Chapter Eleven

There were those in and around Forever, Cody among them, who felt that Miss Joan really did have eyes in the back of her head. How else would she be aware of every little thing that was happening, often simultaneously, in her crowded diner? It was a given that nothing got past the titian-haired woman with the deep, penetrating hazel eyes.

Today was no different. Cody had barely made it in through the diner door at lunchtime—always an incredibly busy time of day for Miss Joan—before she was suddenly next to him. He'd come in to get food to go and to express Devon's thanks for the sirloin sandwich the woman had sent over last night.

"Missed you this morning," Miss Joan informed him, startling Cody. "When you didn't come in for your morning coffee, I thought you'd decided to stay home and lend that little girl a hand with her baby."

Cody congratulated himself for giving no indication that the woman had caught him off guard. "No, actually, Devon made coffee for all of us this morning." He added tactfully, "It was almost as good as yours, Miss Joan."

Far from acting slighted, the owner of the diner

was very displeased by what he was telling her. "You've got that girl making coffee?" Miss Joan asked him in an accusatory tone. "What else are you having her do?"

Cody deflected the blame easily. "No, she insisted, Miss Joan. By the time I got down to the kitchen, Devon had already made coffee and she had breakfast going, as well. She said she needed to do that not to feel like a charity case."

Cody held his breath, waiting for the older woman's reaction. Miss Joan was nothing if not unpredictable. Finally, the woman slowly nodded her head in approval. "Spunky. I like that."

He breathed a silent sigh of relief. "She wanted me to thank you for sending over that dinner last night. She really enjoyed it."

He could see the older woman was pleased, even though she waved the words away. Miss Joan drew him over to the counter, and then made her way behind it. In a second, she was filling customers' coffees.

"How's she doing today?" she asked.

Cody smiled. "She looks a lot better than she did when I brought her into the clinic." Anything would have been an improvement over that.

"Well, I should hope so," Miss Joan said sharply. "And the baby?"

"Sounds happy, looks healthy." He knew that Miss Joan appreciated brevity. She didn't like wading through miles of words to reach the answers she wanted.

"You got everything you need?" she questioned. "Because I had Henry pick up a couple of packs of disposable diapers to tide her over." To prove it, she took out the packs from behind the counter and placed them in front of Cody.

The woman was a godsend. "She could definitely use those," he agreed.

Miss Joan's next question came right out of the blue and caught him off guard, although it did reinforce his belief that the woman was all-seeing. "What's the baby sleeping in?"

"Right now, a drawer," he told her, watching for her reaction.

The pencil-thin eyebrows narrowed above her piercing hazel eyes. "A what?" she demanded.

Cody tried to make it sound more accommodating. "We put blankets and a sheet into a drawer. It was the best I could come up with on the spur of the moment. It's been years since there was a crib set up in the house," he told her by way of an excuse.

Miss Joan pressed her thin lips together and he knew that what he'd just told her was not making her happy, but there wasn't anything he could do about it. His father had gotten rid of the crib years ago, when Cassidy turned five.

Just as he decided that she wasn't going to say anything else to him, Miss Joan instructed, "All right, stop by here on your way home tonight."

"Why?" He'd planned on not wasting any time and just going directly to the ranch the minute he clocked out at the sheriff's office.

"Because I just told you to," Miss Joan retorted. "Didn't your father ever teach you not to question your elders?"

"I guess he must've skipped that lesson," Cody told her with a grin.

Miss Joan pinned him with a look. "Don't give me any snappy answers, young man. Just be here." She waved him over to one of the waitresses. "Now, tell Margarita your order and go get back to work," she told him, and then specified, "Pronto."

"Yes, ma'am," Cody replied, turning toward the waitress she had pointed out.

Like a woman on a mission, Miss Joan went back to her small office at the rear of the diner. She had phone calls to make.

CODY PULLED HIS packed truck up right in front of the house. This would definitely *not* have been a good day for riding Flint to work.

He eased his way out from behind the steering wheel, barely being able to wiggle passed the various items that had been stuffed into his truck. As it was, there wasn't enough space leftover in the cab for an oversize cough drop.

Miss Joan had been exceptionally busy playing the sharp-tongued fairy godmother.

Closing the driver's side door, Cody decided to leave everything Miss Joan's husband and step-grandson had loaded onto his truck. He would need help getting the things out and, since he didn't see any other vehicle in front of the house except for Devon's beaten-up truck, he assumed that the others hadn't come home yet.

So, for the time being, he left everything where it was, except for the diapers. Those he took in with him.

After tucking one bag under his arm, he unlocked

the front door. Ordinarily, the door was rarely locked. Safety around here was not an issue. But because he'd left Devon on her own with the baby, he felt justified in taking the extra precaution.

"Hi, I'm home," he called out, closing the door behind him.

He thought it best to announce himself—just in case. After accidentally walking in on Devon when she was breastfeeding the baby, he didn't want to take a chance on that happening again. She had enough to deal with without thinking that she had temporarily thrown her lot in with a voyeur.

"Devon?" Cody called out, although not too much louder. He didn't want to risk waking up the baby if she'd fallen asleep somewhere close by, such as the living room.

But Layla wasn't in the living room. Neither was Devon.

Because he was focused on finding her and her baby, Cody didn't realize until he'd taken several steps into the living room that there was something else missing, as well.

The chaos that had been in the room as he'd left this morning was no longer there. Haphazardly thrown shirts and jackets, books and notepads, actually *all* the things that had been strewn around were no longer evident. In their place, order had been restored.

Out of all of them, Connor was the orderly one, but in the last few weeks, he'd been too busy with calving season on the ranch to pay attention to the growing piles in the living room that had all but taken on a life of their own.

Everything was neatly stacked, folded or just plain put away.

Cody made his way through the room, looking around uncertainly.

"Connor?" he called out, even though he hadn't seen Connor's truck parked anywhere outside. "Are you home?"

This time, he got a response, although it wasn't from Connor or anyone else in his family. Instead, Devon walked into the room looking fairly pleased with herself.

"You're home early," she observed. "I didn't think you'd be back for another hour.

He noticed that she had on a pair of jeans and a blouse that looked vaguely familiar. Her midnight black hair was loose and seemed to swing about her face as she walked. He had to force himself not to stare.

Another man might have said something about wanting to rush back home to see how she was doing, but Cody was nothing if not honest. His father had once observed that he didn't think Cody *knew* how to lie.

"Everybody was fixated on having me go home early, so I finally took the hint."

"Everybody?" Devon questioned, not exactly sure who he was referring to.

"Miss Joan mostly," he clarified. "But the sheriff, too. He told me I'd do more good at home than at the office." He looked around. "Did Connor come home during the day?" He thought that would be odd because, at breakfast, Connor had mentioned having to stay out all day.

"No, why?" she asked uneasily.

Was this about the living room? She'd wanted to do something nice and she'd wanted to keep busy, but maybe she'd overstepped her boundaries. She certainly didn't want to annoy Cody and the others or offend them for some reason.

Cody gestured around the room. "It's neat," he said, clearly confused.

She watched his expression as she explained. "Oh, that—well, I thought since the baby was asleep and I had time on my hands…"

To her relief, he didn't look angry, just mystified. "If you had time on your hands, you should have taken a nap, too," he told her.

Devon shook her head. "Not my style," she said, and then hastily assured Cody, "Don't worry, I didn't get rid of anything. I just organized it. The books are on shelves in the bookcase and the clothes are hung up in the hall closet."

He looked around the room again, clearly impressed. It hadn't been this uncluttered in a long time. "You did a nice job," he said belatedly.

She beamed but made no comment. Instead, she pointed to the two large bags he was still holding in his hands. "What's that?" she asked.

He'd almost forgotten. "Oh right. Miss Joan sent over some disposable diapers."

The expression on her face couldn't have been brighter than if he had just presented her with a five-carat diamond. Still, she was a little wary. "Why would she do that?"

"Because she's Miss Joan," he told her, adding, "It doesn't get any more complicated than that, trust me. When she thinks something needs to be done or taken care of, she just does it."

For now, Devon set aside her suspicions. "Really? That's wonderful," she cried.

Now that her guard was down, at least temporarily, Devon looked like a kid on Christmas morning, he thought. "She sent other things," he told her.

This was beginning to feel like a dream, Devon thought. Who *were* these people anyway? She looked at him a little uncertainly.

"What other things?" she asked.

"They're in the truck." He decided not to wait for help. After all, he wasn't exactly a weakling. He just had to exercise caution in lifting some things out. "I'll bring them in," he told her.

Within a few minutes, the newly uncluttered living room was filled with a different sort of clutter. There was a large box of baby clothes, ranging from newborn to twelve months old, a bassinet that looked as if it had come straight out of a fairy tale and a box of toys of various sizes, most of them stuffed.

It was too good to be true.

She could feel her eyes welling up as she ran her hand ever so lightly over the bassinet. Since it was mounted on wheels, it would be easy for her to move to any part of the guest room as well as into the living room and the kitchen if she needed to.

"This is wonderful," she said in a small, halting voice, afraid to speak up because she thought her voice would crack. "Where did you get all this?"

"Miss Joan is very resourceful," he told her matter-of-factly. "And," he added, "there have been a number of babies born in Forever in the last few years. Miss Joan just knew who to call.

"Technically," he specified, "these are all on loan—except for the diapers, of course."

"I don't care if they're on loan," Devon told him. "The fact that I can use them even for a little while is just wonderful," she said, tearing up completely.

Cody noticed immediately. He'd heard her voice crack. Nothing made him feel more helpless than tears. "Oh, hey, you're not going to cry, are you?"

"No," she said and then promptly had several fat tears go cascading down both of her cheeks.

Unable to talk for a moment, she waved away any words that he was going to say. She knew she couldn't answer him.

It took her a moment to catch her breath.

At a loss, not knowing what else to do, Cody took her in his arms and just held her, saying nothing. He didn't want her to feel he was trying to intrude on her feelings or take advantage of her. He just wanted her to know that he was there for her, no matter what she needed.

Regaining control over herself, Devon took a deep breath and stepped back after a second. Cody handed her his handkerchief and waited until she'd fully composed herself.

"It's okay," he told her. "Just take your time. There's no hurry."

She pressed her lips together, still trying to regain control and to sound coherent. It took her another couple of minutes.

When Devon could finally talk, she told Cody,

"It's just that no one's ever done anything like this for me. Ever."

"Well, they should have." It was all that he would allow himself to say. He knew that if he gave voice to what he was feeling, if he said the negative things he was thinking about the man who had skipped out on her, it would do her no good to hear them.

Because he needed something to divert her attention for a moment, Cody directed it toward the bassinet.

"Let's get this into your room and see how the princess likes her new sleeping accommodations," he suggested. "Anything has to be an improvement over that drawer."

Devon wiped away her tears, grateful to Cody for what he was attempting to do. "Oh, I don't know," she said, playing along. "The drawer wasn't such a bad idea. Actually, I think it was kind of sweet, seeing her in it. And," she added, "it was definitely original."

"Well, maybe not that original," Cody admitted. "Before they found out about me, my parents really weren't expecting another baby. Cole was in the only crib they had and they didn't think putting both of us in that one crib was a good idea, so for about the first month, until they could find a second-hand crib for me, my dad had me sleeping in what used to be the sock drawer."

She laughed, charmed. "Thank you for this."

"Hey, don't thank me," he told her. "Thank Miss Joan. This was all her doing. She knew who to call and nobody says no to Miss Joan." He winked. "It just isn't done."

"Well, tell her I think she's wonderful," Devon

said and then added, "And I think you're wonderful, as well."

Overwhelmed with gratitude and just plain happiness, Devon meant to underscore her thanks with a kiss to his cheek. But this time, just as she was about to brush her lips against it, Cody turned his head to say something to her.

Which was how her lips wound up on his.

To say that Cody was surprised to find himself in that position would have been a huge understatement. He more than half expected Devon to pull back.

But she didn't.

Once what had happened registered with her, instead of quickly pulling away and mumbling some sort of embarrassed, half-coherent apology, Devon surprised them both by continuing the contact.

And just like that, the kiss transformed to one that was meant to be a person-to-person kiss rather than just a quick, fleeting peck on the cheek.

The moment the kiss deepened, it became a genuine kiss.

For just a moment, she let herself go—all the pent-up feelings, anxieties, emotions, *everything* that was inside her rose within her chest and found release in the timeless contact.

Stunned, Cody was afraid that if he reacted accordingly, he'd scare her off.

But then he decided to risk it by folding his arms around her and drawing her just a hint closer. Her mouth tasted sweet, sweeter than anything he could recall ever having sampled.

If he continued on this route, emotions might just

spike, rising to a level where they were not easily kept in check.

So it was with the greatest reluctance that he forced himself to break contact and end the kiss.

"Sorry," he murmured, "I didn't mean to take advantage of you."

"You didn't," she whispered.

Then, afraid of what he might think of her for needing him like this, Devon stepped back. "I made dinner," she told him. "I hope Connor won't mind."

"Mind?" he repeated. "He'll be relieved and thrilled. Connor hates cooking. He just does it out of necessity." He confided, "We all do. But I didn't bring you here to clean and cook,"

"I know that," she replied. "But I didn't know what else to do with myself."

He smiled at Devon. "The word *rest* comes to mind."

"I did," she told him. "But I couldn't do that all day," she protested.

Cody laughed. "I know several people who could argue that point with you." He was about to say something else, but Layla began to cry. "Is she hungry?" he asked.

Devon checked the baby's bottom first. "No. You brought those diapers home just in time," she told him.

"Need help?" he asked.

She was about to tell him that she could do it herself and then had second thoughts. "An extra set of hands might be nice," she told him.

"Funny you should say that. I just happen to have a set," he said with a grin, holding his hands up in the air the way a surgeon might when entering an operating room. "Let's get your daughter dry."

Devon could only smile at that. Smile and fervently pray that she wouldn't wake up too soon.

# Chapter Twelve

"Well, it's official," Connor declared, pushing back his empty plate on the dining room table. For a moment, he sat there, feeling too full to even move. For once he'd eaten too much, something he rarely did. But it had definitely been worth it. "You have a place here for as long as you want, Devon." A sigh of contentment escaped his lips. "That has to be one of the best meals I can remember ever having eaten. Where did you learn how to cook that way?" he asked her.

Color crept up into Devon's cheeks. The oldest McCullough's compliment had embarrassed her even as it pleased her.

"Necessity," Devon replied simply. "My mother taught me how to make do with whatever I found in the refrigerator and the pantry. Adding a few spices and flavored breadcrumbs to the mix can really work miracles if you do it right," she said modestly.

"Well, whatever it is that you're doing, keep right on doing it," Cole told her, joining the chorus of approval.

Cody had enjoyed the meal as much as everyone else had, maybe even more, but he really didn't want Devon to feel obligated or put upon. "C'mon, people, you don't want to make her feel like she's got to keep cooking for us," he protested.

"I'm with Cody. You're going to make her feel like an indentured servant who can't say no," Cassidy said.

"No, really, I don't mind," Devon said. "It makes me feel that I'm at least paying you back in some small way for all your kindness," she told the others as she started to gather up the dinner plates and silverware. "Besides, I like cooking."

"Well, you can go on cooking for us if you don't mind doing it, but no way are you going to wash the dishes after the meal's over," Cody informed her sternly, moving the stacked dishes away from her.

"Cody's right," Cassidy told her. "Cooking is a talent—washing dishes is just grunt work."

"Glad you feel that way," Cody told his sister. "As I remember, it's your turn in the kitchen." He pushed the dishes in front of Cassidy.

Cassidy pursed her lips, frowned and then, with a sigh, got to her feet as she picked up the stack of dirty dishes.

"No, really," Devon insisted, "I don't mind cleaning up after a meal."

"You might not," Connor allowed, "but we do. Cassidy's right. Cooking is more than enough. Cleaning up would turn you into a maid and you're our guest," Connor informed her.

The discussion was abruptly cut short by the McCulloughs' tiniest guest. Devon had wheeled Layla's bassinet into the dining room, placing it in the far corner so that she'd be able to hear her daughter when she woke up.

Which she did.

"I believe that settles the argument," Cody quipped with a laugh. Not waiting for Devon to cross to the bassinet, he got there ahead of her. "And what's your complaint?" he asked the infant, looking down at the little puckered face.

"Well, I fed her and changed her just before dinner so my guess is that she probably just wants attention," Devon speculated.

"Then attention is what this little princess is going to get," Cody declared.

Leaning over the bassinet, he deftly picked up the baby. Layla settled down the moment he had her against his shoulder.

"If I didn't know any better, I'd say that it looks like she's taken a shine to you," Cole told his brother.

"Why not?" Cassidy spoke up. "They're about the same age."

"Don't pay any attention to them, Princess," Cody told the infant in his arms. "They're just jealous because you like me better than them."

Infants weren't supposed to be able to recognize anyone and most likely it was gas that was responsible for that funny little twist of her lips, but Devon chose to believe otherwise.

"She does seem to light up around you," Devon agreed, smiling.

*And Layla isn't the only one*, she added silently. She shut out the thought since she was in a vulnerable place right now and Cody was being nice to her. There was no reason to make anything of that. She knew what could happen if she wasn't vigilant about her feelings.

Out loud she told Cody, "I guess she senses how kind you are."

"Or maybe she just thinks you need a friend your own age," Cole cracked.

Cody turned his back on Cole, ignoring his brother. The baby had all his attention. "Don't pay any attention to him, Princess. He just likes to hear himself talk."

"C'mon, sweetie, it's time to give you your first bath," Devon told her daughter as she took the infant from Cody.

"A bath?" Cole echoed, concerned. "Isn't she a little small for that?"

"Not really." Devon laughed. "I'm bathing her in the bathroom sink, not the bathtub," she assured Cody's brother. Seeing the somewhat-concerned looks on all their faces, she assured the others, "She'll be fine. I'm going to be in complete control."

"Want some help?" Cody volunteered.

She wanted to tell him that she didn't need help, that she had this covered, but that was just her independent streak talking. The truth of it was that every new thing she attempted with her daughter had her trembling inside.

So rather than turn Cody down, Devon flashed a relieved smile at him and accepted his offer. "That would be very nice of you."

"Nice is my middle name," he told her in a low voice, hoping not to be overheard by any of his siblings.

He hoped in vain. Cole and Cassidy rolled their eyes in response to his comment. Connor merely shook his head. But since none of them said anything in response, Cody counted himself ahead in the game.

"Good to know," Devon replied before pushing the bassinet back into the guest room as Cody followed her with the baby.

After moving the bassinet into a corner, she turned around to face Cody. There was something so very heartwarming about seeing him cradling her daughter in his arms.

*Snap out of it, Devon. No more entanglements, remember?*

Squaring her shoulders, she told Cody, "Why don't you continue to hold her while I get everything ready?"

"Don't have to ask me twice," he answered. Layla looked perfectly fine with this arrangement, Devon couldn't help thinking.

She swiftly laid out the baby's new diaper and a change of clothing, thanks to the box of clothes Miss Joan had collected for Layla.

With that ready, she went to the bathroom sink and ran the water, making sure it was just the right temperature for the infant. Aside from a large, fluffy towel, she also got a cup ready, placing it nearby.

"Okay," Devon said, taking the baby from Cody, "Time to make a water baby out of you," she told Layla as she laid the infant on her bed.

She removed the baby's clothing, secretly relieved that Layla had seen fit not to leave any unexpected deposits in her fresh diaper.

Cody watched her as she got the baby ready for her bath. "You sure you didn't have any younger brothers or sisters?" he asked her.

"Nope," she verified, "it was always just me."

She seemed to be too confident about what she was doing to be a novice, he thought. "But you babysat a lot of infants, right?"

"No. Why would you say that?"

Slowly immersing Layla's lower half into the water, she gently splashed a little water along the baby's tummy. Layla made a noise that sounded as if she liked what was happening.

"You just seem very comfortable with all this. I thought maybe you'd done it before." And then he shrugged. "I guess you're just a natural."

She laughed. For a second, she considered letting his impression stand, but then she thought better of it. She didn't want him thinking she was something she wasn't. There'd been enough of that in her life with Jack. She couldn't play any games, even if they were the kind that was totally inconsequential.

Tilting the baby back a little against one arm, she cupped her other hand and allowed a little warm water to wet the fringe of dark hair on Layla's head.

"Look in my purse," she prompted. When he glanced at her curiously, she added, "It's on the desk."

He wasn't sure why she wanted him to look in her purse, but he retrieved it and then opened it the way she instructed. Inside was an extremely worn, dog-eared copy of a paperback book written by a popular pediatrician.

"That was a new book when I got it," she told him when he held up the book to make sure it was what she'd wanted him to find. "I was determined to be the very best mother I could be—and to be as prepared as possible for all the bumps and hiccups that were bound to come up in the first few months of this little partnership," she told him. Devon leaned over and lightly kissed the top of her baby's wet head.

Devon made a face, wrinkling her nose.

"What?" he questioned.

"Shampoo," she explained. "I guess I didn't get all of it out. Here, I'll tilt her back again. Fill that cup up and pour it along the back of her head," she instructed.

The directions sounded awkward, but he got the general gist of it. Very carefully, he allowed a stream of warm water to cascade along the back of her hair.

A tiny squeal pierced the air.

Devon raised her eyes, meeting Cody's. "I think she likes it."

A wide, wide smile curved Cody's mouth. He seemed to all but radiate pleasure. "You know, I think that you're right."

She had the infant cradled against one arm while she gently used a washcloth to pass along the baby's body with the other. She could see he appeared surprised at how well she was doing.

"I practiced with a doll," she confessed. She didn't add that Jack had ridiculed her for it. She should have known then that it wasn't going to work out for them.

"Well, it looks like it paid off," Cody told her. "You've got it covered."

The compliment pleased her more than she thought it would.

"I do, don't I?" she responded. "But I'd still like to know I've got backup, just in case," she told him.

"I'm not going anywhere," he assured her.

Between the two of them, Layla received her first bath—and got through it with flying colors.

Lifting the infant out of the water, Devon wrapped the large white towel around her, gently patting the baby's body.

Her eyes met Cody's. "We did it," she declared happily. She placed Layla on the bed and then patted her completely dry.

"*You* did it," Cody corrected. He let out the water. "I was just a bystander."

"You were more than that," she told him. There was gratitude in her eyes as she looked at him. "You were moral support."

Having dried off the baby, Devon diapered Layla and then slipped on a onesie that Miss Joan also had sent over with Cody.

"Okay, you're clean, changed and fed," she pronounced. "Time for bed, little girl."

She placed the infant back into the bassinet, and then went into the bathroom to make sure everything had been cleaned up. To her surprise, Cody had missed nothing. Everything was back in its place. The man was incredible, she caught herself thinking.

When she came back into the bedroom, she found that Cody was sitting on the edge of the bed, gently pushing the bassinet to and fro. The motion created a soothing sensation.

Devon paused over the bassinet and peered in. Layla's eyes were closed and she looked very peaceful. The infant was asleep.

She glanced back up at Cody. "You're an absolute wizard," she told him.

"The bassinet has wheels," Cody responded. "They did the hard part."

Devon sat down on her bed, suddenly feeling as if the very air had been drained out of her. She hadn't realized that she was this tired. Just remaining upright took effort.

"I really had no idea I was so exhausted," she confessed.

"You put in a full day, making breakfast for all of us as well as dinner," Cody enumerated. "And being a mom, especially a new one, is a full-time job. If you *weren't* exhausted, I would have said there was something seriously wrong with you."

"Then I guess there's nothing wrong with me," Devon told him, "because I can hardly sit up."

"Then go to sleep," he suggested simply.

Cody began to get up so she could do just that. But he found that he couldn't leave. Devon had caught hold of his arm. When he looked at her quizzically, she said, "Don't go yet. Talk to me."

Sitting back down, he acted as if she'd just made the most normal request in the world. "What about?"

A long sigh escaped her lips. "Anything you want." And then, because that was so vague, she got him started. "Tell me about your day."

"It wasn't very exciting," he told her.

She was starting to feel very sleepy—but she still didn't want him to leave. She felt as if he was her good-luck charm.

"Did you get to talk to anybody?" she asked.

"Sure." The sheriff's office could be a very noisy place.

"Then it was exciting," she assured him with a

yawn. Devon settled in against him, surprising Cody when she leaned her head against his shoulder. "Talk," she requested again, and then tempered her plea because she didn't want him feeling like a prisoner in his own house. "Just for a little while longer."

"I'll talk for as long as you want me to," he promised, slipping his arm around her shoulders.

Cody doubted that she even consciously noticed that, although she did seem to curl into him a little bit more, not unlike a kitten seeking shelter.

"Okay, then," he murmured.

Cody started to talk, giving Devon a full report of his earlier interaction with Miss Joan as well as with the sheriff and the other deputies, Joe and Gabe.

He talked slowly, purposefully, stretching out his narrative as much as he could. As he spoke, he tried not to get distracted by the feeling of her hair brushing against his cheek or the scent of what he took to be her perfume, which seemed to be everywhere.

Or maybe that was just her shampoo, he amended. Whatever it was, it was something light and herbal, but he still found it extremely stirring and distracting.

It also made him realize that it had been more than a while since he had socialized with any of the young women in the area who were around his own age.

That had not been a conscious decision. It had evolved on its own because he'd been so busy learning all the ins and outs of his relatively new position as deputy. This while still lending a hand on the ranch whenever Connor got in over his head and needed him and the others.

His life might not have been exciting by anyone's standards, but it definitely could be taxing at times.

The salary he earned as a deputy went into a communal account, along with the money that Cole brought in and whatever Cassidy managed to earn working part-time both at the diner and at Olivia Santiago's law firm as her assistant.

It wasn't an easy life for any of them, but Connor had been there for them when they needed it and they were returning the favor. If not for Connor, they would have been farmed out to foster homes, most likely *separate* foster homes. And though Connor never talked about it, he had given up his dreams in order to keep them all together while running the ranch. The three of them had agreed long ago that they would never be able to actually pay Connor back for what he'd done, but they could damn well try at least.

In a way, this helped Cody understand why Devon insisted on finding a way to pay them back.

Cody realized after a few minutes that he was telling Devon all this, sharing more of his life with her than he had ever done with anyone else outside of the family, besides Miss Joan. But then the older woman had just intuitively known the details without his having to say them.

She always knew everything.

Sharing this with someone else, namely Devon, was a new experience. As soon as he realized what he was doing, he abruptly stopped.

Cody began to rise, trying to gently shift Devon's weight so that she would be lying down in the bed.

But as he started to do so, he heard a little noise of complaint escape her lips. Glancing down at her face, he saw that Devon was still asleep.

Still, he was sure he'd just heard her whisper, "Stay."

Debating, Cody decided to remain just a little longer, at least until she had fallen into a somewhat deeper sleep. After all, he had nowhere to go and nothing pressing to do.

And there were worse things than sitting beside a beautiful, sleeping woman, he thought with a smile.

So Cody remained where he was, sitting on Devon's bed, keeping his arm supportively around her so that she wouldn't just slump forward or fall over.

It occurred to Cody that a lot of people would have considered this to be the perfect ending to a rather hectic day.

A kernel of contentment opened up within him and spread even as darkness tiptoed into the bedroom, wrapping all three of them in a blanket of peace.

Inexplicably, a fresh wave of her shampoo filled his senses. Cody smiled again.

*Perfect.*

## Chapter Thirteen

Without any actual planning or real forethought, Cody found that, over the course of the next few weeks, a routine had fallen into place.

His mornings didn't officially begin until he'd looked in on Layla and her mother. Usually, they were in the kitchen, with Devon effortlessly preparing breakfast for all of them. He always pitched in despite her initial protest. Being around Devon and her baby, even if it was just until he drove off to work, gave Cody something to look forward to the minute he opened his eyes.

He knew that, eventually, this would come to an end, that Devon would one day, most likely soon, announce that she was ready to start forging a life for herself and her daughter somewhere apart from the McCullough household. But that day didn't have to be today—and, as long as it wasn't, he put it out of his mind and just enjoyed each minute as it happened.

Living in the moment took on a whole new, vivid meaning for him.

And all too quickly, it began to feel as if it was always this way, as if Devon and the baby had always been a part of their lives.

A part of *his* life.

And it didn't go unnoticed.

"You're getting too attached," Connor warned him one morning, following him out of the house just as he was about to leave for work.

Cody kept walking, heading for his truck. "No, I'm not," he protested, trying not to sound defensive.

Connor kept pace with him. As Cody opened the door on the driver's side, Connor put his hand on it, temporarily keeping it in place.

"Yeah, you are," Connor contradicted, concerned. "Things change all the time, Cody. You have to be prepared for that."

Cody planted his feet firmly, stubbornly turning to face his older brother. "I'm not twelve, Connor."

"No, you're not," Connor agreed. "Which is why it'll really hurt when she leaves. And she is going to leave, you know that," Connor emphasized. "She's not the type to let things slide and have other people take care of her." He nodded back toward the house. "That's a lady who pays her own way."

Devon was already doing that. There was no reason for her to leave yet, Cody thought, resisting the idea that Connor was expounding upon.

"According to her, she is paying her own way. She's saving us from your cooking," Cody said pointedly.

"Very funny." But Connor wasn't going to let him put up a smoke screen.

Cody tried not to get annoyed. He knew that Connor meant well. But he was getting a little too old to have his older brother meddling in his affairs.

"I know what you're saying—that this is just temporary. But that doesn't mean I can't enjoy it while it lasts," Cody told him.

"Nobody said that," Connor agreed. "Get to work before you're late," he said, waving Cody off and stepping back.

Once at work, since the atmosphere was so relaxed, Cody went on with his search to find the man who had abandoned Devon. He'd managed—working with the little that he had been able to get out of her—to discover the man's name. Jack Tryon. That led him, after a great deal of effort and searching through various databases, to a New Mexico driver's license that had Tryon's picture on it. He circulated the photo, sending it to the various motels in a hundred-mile radius.

He got no hits, but he refused to give up. The man had to turn up somewhere.

"WHAT'S THAT?" DEVON ASKED one afternoon several days later.

Cody had come home early and, as was his habit, his first stop was the kitchen. He liked to hang around, talking to Devon while she prepared dinner.

Devon's question pertained to the bouquet of wild roses that Cody was holding out to her.

Cody flashed an engaging grin. "Most people call them flowers," he quipped.

"I *know* what they are," she said, and then tried again, "but why are you giving them to me?"

"To celebrate," he told her simply, deliberately doling out his answer slowly in small pieces.

"Okay," she allowed. "Are you celebrating anything in particular?"

His grin was irresistible—she found that she didn't stand a chance. "Today marks four weeks since you came here and made mealtime bearable instead of just something to get through."

Rather than laugh at his quip, Devon looked surprised. Since she'd arrived at the ranch, her days had begun to run into one another and she'd lost track of time more than once.

But even so, she had to admit, if only to herself, that she hadn't been this happy in a long, long time. She'd admonished herself, telling herself not to get used to it, but the truth was she just couldn't help it.

His words now were a jarring reminder. "My lord, has it been that long?" she cried.

It felt as if she'd only arrived the day before yesterday. She hadn't meant to take such advantage of them, she thought, the wheels in her head beginning to turn madly.

"Actually," Cody told her, "it feels like time's just glided by."

But Devon didn't see it that way. Still holding the flowers Cody had given her, Devon sank down at the table with a look on her face that Cody could only describe as dazed.

There was almost shock and wonder in her voice as she realized, "I've taken advantage of your hospitality for an entire month."

"No," Cody corrected firmly, "you've made our lives *better* for an entire month." Devon still looked unconvinced. She couldn't possibly be thinking of leaving, he thought nervously. "These are flowers," Cody pointed out, "not an eviction notice. If anyone's taken advantage of anyone, we've taken advantage of you."

The look in her eyes told him that she didn't see it that way. "I should have found a place for Layla and me by now."

"You didn't have the time," he said. "You've been too busy taking care of her and cooking for us," Cody reminded her, adding, "There's no hurry. The invitation to stay on is open-ended," he insisted.

That made her feel worse. "You're just being nice."

"I'm only being practical," Cody insisted. He needed to make her understand. "Having you and Layla here brightens up the place." And then he smiled at her. "I can't even explain exactly why, but there's a lot less bickering going on in this house with you here." He looked at the bouquet in her hands. It had all started with the bouquet. "If the flowers upset you, I'll get rid of them," he offered, about to take them out of her hand.

"No!" Reflexes had her pulling the bouquet out of his reach. "The flowers are beautiful." Devon could count the number of times she'd received flowers from someone on one finger of one hand. This was a first for her. "It just reminds me that I should get busy finding a niche for myself and Layla."

No matter what he said, she couldn't expect Cody and his family to put her up forever.

"And by 'niche' you mean a job," Cody guessed, reading between the lines.

"Exactly."

He could understand how she felt. The inevitable became a little more so to him as he asked, "What did you do before you came here?"

"You mean what did I do for a living back in New Mexico?" she asked.

"Yes. What sort of job did you have?" Maybe if he knew what she'd done for a living he could help her find something in Forever.

"I was a substitute teacher." She'd wanted to teach full-time, but Jack had been selfish with her time, wanting her to be around whenever he felt he needed her. A part-time position allowed her to be available.

Cody noticed a rather wistful expression slip over her face when she said the word *teacher*.

"What?" he coaxed. "You were thinking of something. What was it?"

She debated just waving his question away. Jack had ridiculed her for giving voice to her dreams. But Cody looked genuinely interested, so she took a chance and told him. "I was going to enroll in an online college, get some credits toward my degree. I want to eventually teach at a junior college." And then she shrugged away the notion. "Or I did before something more important lay claim to my time," she added, glancing toward the baby, who was in the bassinet, having a wonderful time entertaining herself by playing with her toes.

Cody nodded. "Sounds like a noble idea," he told Devon. His reaction totally surprised her. "You can still do that here. Connor has a computer he doesn't use unless he absolutely has to. It's set up in the den. I'm sure he'll let you use it. And, on the plus side, you have a lot of babysitters to watch Layla for you while you take your classes."

Excitement warred with common sense. "I can't

ask you or your brothers and sister to do that," she told him.

"You're not," Cody pointed out to her. "We're volunteering."

She really wanted to take him up on that, but it wouldn't be right. "You mean you're volunteering for them."

"Only because they don't know about this plan of yours," he replied simply. "Once they know, they'll be only too happy to get on board."

He was painting a very rosy picture, but she couldn't allow herself to get swept away. She'd survived only by having both feet planted in the real world. "I still need to get a place of my own."

"Nobody's arguing with that. It just doesn't have to be today—or tomorrow," he pointed out.

She felt herself waffling. "But I've already imposed more than enough."

"Nobody's complaining," he told her, "and no, you haven't. Look, I know that you've pretty much been on your own a lot and maybe the concept is hard for you to grasp, but *this* is what family and friends do— they're there for each other, they make life easier for each other." Trying his best to get through to her, he underscored, "Let us help."

Didn't he understand? "You already have."

The corners of his mouth curved in an appealing smile. "Let us help more."

Devon sighed. It would be so easy just to let him take care of things for her. But she knew better than that. She couldn't allow herself to depend on anyone too much—that was how she'd wind up getting hurt.

"There is no arguing with you, is there?" she asked Cody.

"Oh, there's arguing," he contradicted. "But if you mean winning, then no, there's not. You can argue all you want, but in the end the house wins. In this case," he told her with a smile, "the 'house' means me—and the others."

She shook her head, knowing it was futile to keep trying to persuade him, at least for now. But she was still also afraid to allow herself to believe things could be this simple, this easy. For now, she turned her attention to dinner. "How do you feel about chicken parmesan?"

"Passionate," Cody answered, tongue in cheek.

Her eyes smiled as she said, "Then lucky for you, that's what I'm making."

In his opinion, that wasn't why he was lucky.

"BUT WHERE ARE we going?" Devon asked as Cody ushered her toward his truck.

It was Saturday and while he wasn't working today, he still seemed determined to go on an unannounced outing with her.

"I thought you might want a break from everything," Cody said matter-of-factly. "You've been cooped up in the house much too long so I'm taking you into town. Think of this as a field trip," he advised.

She'd come outside with Cody because she'd thought he wanted to show her something, She wasn't prepared to just take off like this.

"But what about the baby?"

"Cassidy and Cole have watched you enough to

know what to do with Layla for a few hours." Opening the passenger door, he helped her up into the seat as he spoke. "She'll be fine."

Devon twisted around in her seat as Cody slipped the metal tongue into the seat belt slot. "I'm not worried about her. I'm worried about them."

"Don't be." Quickly, he rounded the hood and got in on the driver's side. "Don't even think about the house or the things you need to do." He buckled up quickly. "Just think recreation."

She looked at him suspiciously. Something was off. "What are you up to?" she asked.

He thought of a number of excuses to give her, things to mislead her for the time being. But he'd never been one for lies, even little white ones. So he told her the truth—or at least the partial truth— as he drove into town. "I thought I'd take you to see Miss Joan, seeing as how you two didn't get to visit much when she came to the clinic after the docs fixed you up."

Devon took in a deep breath, trying to steady the onslaught of nerves that had suddenly materialized out of nowhere. Miss Joan had already done a great deal for her. How could she ever thank the woman for everything she'd done for a stranger?

"SHE'S HELPED ME so much. What do I say to her?" she asked Cody when they arrived at the diner half an hour later.

"'Hi' comes to mind. Don't worry, she'll take it from there," he assured her. After getting out, he opened the door for Devon and helped her out.

Devon took a tighter hold of Cody's arm than he'd

expected. It was probably the closest thing to a tourniquet he'd ever experienced, he thought.

"If you say so," Devon murmured, her eyes all but fixed on the entrance to the diner.

Cody leaned his head in so she was able to hear him. "You've met her. You know she doesn't bite."

Devon tossed her head, her hair brushing along her shoulders. "I know that," she murmured, still holding on to his arm as hard as she could.

The moment she walked into the diner, Devon realized that he wasn't bringing her there to say hello to Miss Joan or even to undergo the woman's scrutiny. He'd brought her there because Miss Joan had instructed him to. One look at the crammed diner and it became apparent that the woman had finally gotten the word out to the people she wanted to reach. They had all turned out and came bearing gifts. This wasn't a command performance, Devon realized belatedly. As improbable as it seemed, this was a baby shower.

As soon as he'd opened the door for Devon, she saw the balloons and the various other decorations. A look of delight passed over her face even as the next moment she seemed to freeze in place.

"You didn't," she breathed.

Taking hold of her arm, he steered her across the threshold and into the diner. "Nope, *I* didn't. Miss Joan did," he said, setting her straight.

Why would the woman do this? Devon couldn't help wondering. Why would Miss Joan put herself out for someone she didn't even know?

That question, along with half a dozen others, throbbed in Devon's head as she allowed herself to be led into the heart of the diner.

"Cody?" she said uncertainly.

"Just keep walking," he coaxed. "One foot in front of the other. It gets easier."

She felt as if her head was spinning. There were boisterous voices all swimming into one continuous noise. "What *is* all this?" Devon cried, not knowing where to look first.

"It's your baby shower," Olivia Santiago said as she came around to Devon's other side, ushering her in and acting as her unofficial guide.

"But—but I'm a stranger," Devon protested, not knowing what to make of these people who were so different from anyone she was accustomed to. Baby showers were thrown by friends, by family, none of which these people were to her.

It still felt enchanted, she couldn't help thinking.

"A stranger's just a friend you haven't met yet," Ramona, the sheriff's sister, told her, joining the growing circle around the new mother.

Devon was still having trouble wrapping her head around what was going on.

She looked toward the woman standing at the counter. Miss Joan. Their eyes met and then Miss Joan came forward, smiling a greeting at her.

"Welcome to your baby shower," Miss Joan told her, a regal smile of welcome on her lips.

Unable to contain herself, Devon just started talking. "But you already sent me all those baby clothes and things." Her point was that there was no need for a shower, but something kept her from saying the words.

"Those were hand-me-downs," Miss Joan informed her, beckoning her over to a table that was piled high with gifts. "Every baby deserves to have some brand-new things of her own," she maintained. "Sit," she instructed, pointing to the chair before she waved over one of her waitresses to bring Devon something to drink.

"And don't worry about a thing," Miss Joan told her, continuing. "This is about that sweet little baby—and her mama," she added pointedly, looking at Devon. She had picked out a few items that every new mother needed in order to preserve her own identity, but there was time enough for Devon to unwrap those things later, Miss Joan thought. Right now, the young woman needed to just sit back, relax and enjoy herself.

Miss Joan's eyes narrowed into thin hazel beams as she focused on Cody. "You can make yourself scarce now, Deputy. Someone will come to get you when it's time to load all the gifts onto the truck and take them back to the ranch for the new mama."

Devon turned to look at him, a sliver of panic slicing through her. "You're not staying?"

Cody glanced at Miss Joan. The latter's expression remained firm. "Apparently not."

"Sorry, dear. I'm old-fashioned," Miss Joan informed her, even as she shooed Cody out. "Baby showers are strictly for the softer sex."

On his way out, Cody laughed. Softer sex. As if that described Miss Joan in any manner. But he knew better than to say that out loud, even as she gave him a piercing look.

"Something funny, Deputy?" Miss Joan asked.

"Not a thing, Miss Joan," he told her.

Cassidy was part of the gathering, having managed to get here just a hair's breadth ahead of them. He waved her over to sit beside Devon. When she took her seat, he looked at Devon.

"See you later," he promised just before he left.

Devon watched him exit the diner and desperately wanted to go with him.

## Chapter Fourteen

In an effort to kill time until the baby shower was over and he could take Devon and her gifts back to the ranch, Cody decided to swing by the general store. He figured it was his turn to stock up on basic groceries and supplies anyway.

Since that hardly took any time at all, once he had deposited the groceries into his truck, Cody stopped by the sheriff's office next, but it was even slower there than it normally was during the week. After talking to Gabe, the lone deputy who was on duty this weekend—and being unable to return to the diner, which was technically closed because of the shower—Cody went to the only other place left in Forever where he felt he could kill a little time. Murphy's Saloon.

There was a tacit agreement of long standing between Miss Joan and the three Murphy brothers who owned and ran the saloon that the diner wouldn't serve any alcohol and Murphy's wouldn't serve any food beyond the accepted staples of all bars: pretzels and peanuts.

But that was all right with Cody. He wasn't hungry. He was just at a loose end.

The oldest Murphy brother, Brett, was tending bar and he looked up in surprise when he saw Cody walk in.

"Been a long time," Brett commented as he made his way over to the far end where Cody had parked himself. "What'll it be, Cody?" he asked.

"Got any coffee?" Cody asked. He half expected to have Brett tell him "no."

Brett looked at him thoughtfully for a moment, as if debating his answer. And then he said, "Well, that all depends."

"On what?" Cody asked. Had there been a change in policy?

Brett continued massaging the counter with his cloth, buffing it to a high gloss. "On whether you're asking for yourself or acting as a spy on behalf of Miss Joan."

"For myself," Cody answered. "But I know for a fact that she wouldn't begrudge you serving coffee to your customers if they were trying to sober up." The woman always put safety first.

Brett looked amused. "You do realize that in order to sober up, you'd have to have been drinking first, right?" he pointed out.

Cody shrugged. Had he been interested in drinking, he would have ordered a drink. But it was far too early to cut the edge off the day that way. "Yeah, well, let's just skip that part."

Brett nodded agreeably. Going behind the counter, he picked up the pot of coffee he kept for himself, poured some into a mug and then brought over the pitch-black brew. He placed it in front of Cody.

"You waiting on the baby shower to be over?" he

asked as he set a small container of milk and a sugar bowl beside the mug.

"Yeah." Cody just availed himself of a light dusting of sugar. "How'd you know?" The baby shower at Miss Joan's was possibly the last thing he would have thought Brett knew about.

"Because that's where Alicia is," Brett answered, referring to his wife. "As a matter of fact, that's where all of Forever's women are as far as I can tell." He frowned ever so slightly as he looked off in the general direction of the diner. "Seems almost too eerily quiet without them, doesn't it?"

Cody merely shrugged in response, not really wanting to agree with Brett, not because it wasn't true, but because saying so would have been admitting something to the bartender that he hadn't admitted to himself yet. That he missed the sound of a particular woman's voice.

Brett smiled knowingly. He didn't need any verbal confirmation. "Kind of funny how quick we get used to having them around, isn't it?"

Cody raised his eyes to Brett's. "Are you trying to tell me something?"

Brett's smile just widened a little more. "Nothing you don't already know," he replied.

This was a small town and people talked. Sometimes way too much in Cody's opinion. He didn't want rumors going around about Devon. He had a feeling that it could be way too easy for some of the good people of Forever—well-meaning though they might be—to read between the lines and create scenarios that weren't true.

"Devon's talking about getting her own place as

soon as the baby's a little older." That really had nothing to do with it, but he thought it sounded good.

Brett focused on what he felt was the important part. "So she's staying on in Forever."

Lord, he hoped so. But out loud Cody merely said, "For now."

A look he couldn't quite read passed over Brett's face. "If I were you, I'd make it worth her while."

Cody raised an eyebrow. "What's that supposed to mean?"

"Just about anything you want it to," Brett replied guilelessly.

Cody decided it was best not to take the conversation any further. Finishing off his coffee, he put the mug back on the counter and asked Brett, "What do I owe you for the coffee?"

The expression on Brett's face was the soul of innocence. "Nothing." He shrugged, taking back the mug and passing his cloth along the counter again. "I don't sell coffee here."

Cody laughed shortly. The man's secret was safe with him. "Thanks."

Leaving, he got back into his truck and drove it back to the diner. Cody parked the vehicle across the street and decided to set up camp and wait it out. He felt the shower couldn't go on much longer.

He was right.

Forty-five minutes later, the doors of the diner opened and several of the women who had attended the baby shower came down the steps.

That was his cue, Cody thought, getting out of the truck. Politely nodding at the women and exchanging a few words with Ramona, the town vet and the sheriff's sister, as she came out of the diner next, he made his way inside the restaurant.

He found Devon sitting at a table positioned smack-dab in the center of the diner. There was another table behind her and it was piled high with all sorts of baby furnishings and things designed to make a new mother's life a little easier. The gifts ranged from the very basic to one-of-a-kind items.

"Looks like you cleaned up," Cody remarked, looking over the table.

Devon swung around to face him and it occurred to him that she'd never looked happier to see him.

Or maybe she was just plain happy, he amended.

"I don't know what to say," she confessed, gesturing at the gifts the women had brought to the party. Even Christmas had never looked like this. This was definitely something out of the ordinary.

"You'll think of something," Cody assured her. The other guests who'd attended the party were filing past them and leaving the diner, saying their good-byes. "You ready to go home?" Cody asked her.

*Home.* It had such a nice ring to it. She knew she shouldn't allow herself to get carried away, to feel like this, but she just couldn't help it.

Out loud she said, "Just as soon as we get this into your truck."

At first glance, it looked like a lot, but he'd always been good at organizing things. "No problem. You just sit tight," he told her.

She shook her head. "But I want to help," Devon protested.

Miss Joan came up behind her. "Man wants to do it all, let him do it all," she told Devon. "From what

I hear," she continued, crossing over to the guest of honor, "you've been returning the favor by keeping him and his family well fed."

"Seems like a small thing to do," Devon protested.

"Don't underestimate yourself," Miss Joan warned. Turning to face Cody, the woman waved a thin hand all around the immediate area. "Those are all her things, Cody," the older woman informed him, adding in a no-nonsense voice, "Get busy."

"Yes, ma'am," he replied, doing his best to look solemn. Secretly, he was extremely grateful to her.

Miss Joan had outdone herself. He felt confident that all of this—the shower, the gifts—would go a long way in helping Devon feel more secure about her new life here in Forever.

CODY MOVED QUICKLY as he brought the gifts to his truck. On his last trip, he noticed that Devon had gotten up. He assumed she was getting ready to leave. Instead, he saw her crossing over to Miss Joan. To his surprise, she threw her arms around the older woman.

"Thank you for everything, Miss Joan," Devon murmured.

Knowing Miss Joan's nature, Cody half expected the diner owner to extract herself and say something vague and distant about being physically touched. Instead, as he watched in surprise, Miss Joan not only allowed Devon to hug her, but the woman actually returned the embrace for several seconds before she stepped back and said, "Go home to your baby, Devon. She'll be full grown before you know it."

Brushing aside a tear, Devon nodded in response,

afraid that if she said something, her voice would wind up cracking.

Cody sped up his pace. He took the last of the shower gifts from the table and loaded them onto his truck. Out of the corner of his eye he saw several of the regular customers walking into the diner.

Business as usual had resumed.

Devon was already sitting in the passenger seat when he got in behind the steering wheel. Cody had buckled his seat belt and was just putting the key into the ignition when he heard Devon finally break her silence and speak up.

Glancing at him, she said the obvious. "Miss Joan is an amazing woman."

Cody tactfully suppressed a laugh before responding. "She sure is," he verified.

Devon nodded her head, more to herself than for Cody's benefit. "I wasn't sure what to expect," she confessed.

He turned on the ignition. "So what's your final verdict?" he asked, curious about her impression of the woman.

To his surprise, Devon summed it up rather neatly. "She's scary and sweet at the same time. An angel."

He laughed. "Yeah, I guess that's one description of the lady."

Devon shifted in her seat with her seat belt digging into her shoulder. "Why would Miss Joan do something like that for me?" she asked suddenly. "I mean, I'm nobody to her."

"Because she's Miss Joan," he answered simply. That unadorned statement was the explanation for a good many things the woman had done that remained a mystery to the rest of the town. "And because I think long ago she might have found herself in the same position as you," Cody added.

He paused, and then decided that it might be helpful to Devon if he told her his own story about Miss Joan.

"When my dad died, leaving us orphaned, Connor stepped up to take care of us. If he had gone his own way, Cole, Cassidy and I would have been put into foster care. Lucky for us, he didn't. But Connor didn't manage to take care of us alone. There was always Miss Joan in the wings. She came through with odd jobs for us to do in order to make ends meet. She also fed us on more than one occasion, insisting that if we didn't take the food, she'd only wind up throwing it out because she'd ordered too much."

He smiled to himself. "Nobody can remember Miss Joan miscalculating her inventory. She always knows down to the last serving how much to order, how much to have on hand. Yet for the first couple of years after my dad died, she always seemed to have this 'surplus' lying around." A philosophical smile curved his lips. "Most people in town just think of Miss Joan as this rough-talking guardian angel."

She could add herself to that number. "Well, I think she's wonderful."

She wasn't going to get an argument out of him, Cody thought. "Most of us do, too.'

Twisting farther around in her seat, Devon looked at all the things that she'd gotten as a result of the baby shower. It seemed a little overwhelming now that she looked at it.

"I don't know where you can put all those things," she confessed.

He'd already thought about that. "Don't worry about it, we'll find space."

That seemed to be the go-to catchphrase, she thought. *Don't worry about it.*

The problem was she did.

HER CONCERNS WERE somewhat abated when they reached the house and, rather than make any remarks about her "taking over" the way she feared, Cody's brothers pitched in and helped Cody unload the gifts, which included a brand-new crib that Mrs. Hennessey from the general store had given her, saying that it was a model that someone had ordered and then failed to pick up.

Cole helped to ease the crib out of the truck, bringing the parts into the living room.

"Why don't we set this up upstairs?" Cody suggested. And then he looked at Devon and said, "It's about time the baby had a room of her own so that you can get a good night's sleep."

"But I won't hear her crying if I'm down here," Devon protested.

"Which is why we moved your things upstairs into the bedroom next to the nursery," Connor told her.

She looked from one brother to the other. "You're saying that I can take over two bedrooms?" she asked incredulously.

"Why not?" Connor asked with a shrug. "They're just standing around, empty, going to waste."

Devon's astonished gaze swept over all three brothers. She kept thinking that she was going to wake up at any minute and find out this was all a dream. "You don't mind?" she questioned.

"Why should we mind?" Connor asked. "We're the ones who came up with the suggestion." And then he seemed to read between the lines, guessing why she seemed so wary. "Don't worry, we don't plan to hold you here against your will. Whenever you decide you want to leave, you can leave. But until then, this just seems like the more logical arrangement for everyone."

She didn't know what to say. No one had ever treated her so well or been so thoughtful about her needs and situation.

Not since her mother had passed away.

Tears shimmered in her eyes as she said, "I have to tell you, you all make it very difficult to leave."

Cole and Connor exchanged looks. Connor grinned. "That did cross our minds," he admitted.

She didn't want to break down and cry in front of them. She didn't want them to think she was crazy.

Turning away, she murmured, "I'd better feed and change the baby."

"Already done," Cole informed her proudly.

"Then I'd better get dinner started," Devon said. More tears welled up in her eyes and she hurried into the kitchen quickly.

Connor poked Cody in the ribs and nodded his head in Devon's direction. His message was clear. Devon was definitely a woman in need of comforting.

"Go to her," he told his brother when Cody continued to stand there.

Cody eyed him uncertainly. "Maybe she wants to be alone."

Connor sighed, shaking his head. "Every crying woman needs a shoulder. You don't have to talk. You just have to be there," Connor maintained.

Cody was still undecided about what to do. Which was when Cole pushed him toward the doorway.

He had no choice but to enter the kitchen,

"Are you all right?" he asked Devon quietly.

Rather than answer him, Devon nodded her head.

"Are you sure?" he pressed. He watched the way her shoulders were moving. Connor was right. She was crying. She stopped and turned around to face him. Since there were tears sliding down both cheeks, she couldn't very well protest that she wasn't crying.

Instead, she drew in a ragged breath and said, "These are happy tears."

He could never wrap his mind around that. "How can you tell?"

She tried to smile and didn't quite succeed. "Because I'm happy."

"Okay, you could have fooled me," Cody admitted.

The next thing he knew, Devon had thrown her arms around his neck. "I'm so sorry about this," she sobbed.

"Hey, nothing to be sorry about. You're dealing with a lot here. From where I stand," he told her soothingly, "you're doing a damn fine job of it."

"No, I'm not. If it wasn't for you..." Devon couldn't bring herself to finish her sentence.

"Shh," he said softly, and then told her, "we'll argue about it later." In an effort to soothe her, he held her closer and, ever so slightly, kissed the top of her head.

Devon looked up at him.

The next thing he knew, like a man in a dream, he brought his mouth down to hers.

# Chapter Fifteen

In the next moment, Cody forced himself to step back, murmuring an apology. He wasn't about to say he didn't know what had come over him because he *did* know. He wanted to comfort Devon, just as Connor had said. He wanted her to know she wasn't alone in this. He wanted her not to feel lost.

He wanted her.

Which was why, Cody sternly upbraided himself, he absolutely needed to keep his distance. And that, he realized, would be a challenge—because her room was now next to his.

Devon quickly wiped away her tears with the back of her hand. "I'd better finish getting dinner ready," she said brusquely, turning away from Cody and trying very hard to regain control over herself. She'd slipped, but she wasn't going to allow that to happen again.

For her own survival, she couldn't.

HE HOPED HIS feelings would change, but after two more weeks, they still didn't. If anything, as far as he was concerned, it became more prominent for him.

He was never more aware of Devon's proximity after everything had settled down for the night.

With no effort at all, he came up with a dozen different reasons to look in on Devon, to offer his help with the baby or just to talk. It was a struggle each evening to talk himself out of every one of those excuses. At times he wound up all but barricading himself in his room.

The last thing he wanted was for Devon to feel that he was crowding her—or worse, that because of everything that had transpired, she *owed* him something. It was hard on him, but he forced himself to pull back. That came in the form of his putting in longer hours. He knew that his brothers and sister would handily fill up the space that he left behind. It was in their nature to step up and pitch in whenever Devon needed help.

Eventually, Cody talked himself into believing that Devon didn't even notice what he was doing—except perhaps, that she might feel less hemmed in.

Each day was supposed to grow easier for him. It didn't. After two weeks he still found himself actually missing her despite the fact that he saw Devon every morning before he left the house and every evening after he came home.

It couldn't be helped, Cody thought, but at least his plan was proceeding the way he intended it to. Devon wouldn't feel obliged to him for anything.

There was only one sad side effect of this program of self-denial. Since he'd started keeping his distance from Devon, he found that sleep had become a rather elusive commodity. The main reason for that was because he caught himself straining to hear sounds that would let him know whether or not Devon had gone to sleep or if she was up with the baby.

Moreover, each time he heard any indication of the latter, he had to struggle to keep from getting up and volunteering to take over for her so that at least *she* could get some rest.

It was beginning to take a toll on him. Rather than getting used to this, he found that things were just getting more difficult for him. People were noticing the dark circles under his eyes. Shrugging it off didn't help the basic situation.

Cody had just resigned himself to spending another sleepless night when he thought he heard a light knock on his door.

Sitting up, he stared at the closed door, wondering if he was imagining things. Up until this point, the house had been as quiet as a tomb. Apparently everyone else, including the baby, was asleep.

Curious, Cody got up and opened the door a crack. It allowed him to see that Devon was just turning away from his room. She was wearing an old, oversize T-shirt.

*His* old T-shirt, he realized. Cassidy must have found it somewhere and given it to her. She was obviously using it as her nightgown. The hem only came down halfway on her thighs.

Something tightened in the pit of his stomach.

"Devon?" When she stopped in her tracks and turned around to face him, Cody felt his mouth go dry. "Is something wrong?"

For a moment, she appeared to be waffling, as if she was undecided whether to say something or not. Or maybe the sight of him bare-chested, wearing a pair of old, torn jeans that hung precariously off his hips had rendered her mind blank.

Her internal conflict was short-lived. She squared her shoulders.

Blowing out a deep breath, Devon asked. "Can I come in?"

Because he wanted her to so much, Cody almost asked her if whatever she wanted to talk about couldn't keep until morning.

But something in her expression kept him from asking that. Instead, he stepped back and opened the door farther for her.

"Sure."

Devon took another deep breath, as if to fortify herself, and then crossed his threshold. Before she said a single word, she closed the door behind her.

"Is something wrong with the baby?" Cody asked when she didn't say anything.

Devon shook her head. "No, not the baby," she told him.

"Then what?" He was getting a very uneasy feeling that something was definitely wrong. He might have been avoiding her for her own good, but he didn't want that to keep her from coming to him if something was troubling her. "You can tell me anything," he coaxed.

Rather than pouring out her heart, she looked at him for a long moment.

"Can I?" she questioned.

That threw him. "Sure."

Cody watched her press her lips together as if she was wrestling with a problem. It suddenly occurred to him that she wasn't saying anything because what was bothering her was a woman thing. He told her the only thing he could. "Maybe you'd feel better if I got Cassidy—"

"No," Devon said sharply. She didn't want to talk to Cassidy. She wanted and *needed* to talk to *him*, to have it out with *him*.

Gathering her courage, she asked, "Have I done something to offend you? Because if I have, you have to know that I didn't mean it. I don't know what I did, but I am very sorry." Her eyes met his and she told him with all sincerity, "I would rather die than have that happen."

Cody stared at her, stunned. Where had she gotten that idea?

He stepped forward to put his hands on her shoulders and then caught himself at the last moment. If he touched her, that would lead to something else.

Frustrated, he kept his hands at his sides. "You haven't done anything to offend me," he assured her.

Devon was far from convinced. His answer and his tone of voice only served to confuse her further. This didn't make any sense.

"Then why?" she asked.

"Why what?"

She spelled it out for him. "Why have you been avoiding me?"

Denial was becoming second nature to him. "I haven't been—"

Devon cut him short. She was in no mood to play games.

"Yes, you have. You've been skipping breakfast, staying longer at work and when you actually do come home, if you *do* sit at the table, you don't say anything," she concluded, underscoring her grievances. "And don't," she warned, "tell me that I'm imagining things, because I'm not." She tried to make amends again. "If I somehow hurt your feelings or did something to make you angry, you know I didn't mean to."

"Devon—" he began, searching for some way to reassure her while still maintaining the distance he felt was necessary for his own good "—you haven't done anything."

Frustration clawed at her. Devon felt as if she was going around in circles. "Then why won't you talk to me anymore?" she asked.

This was hard for her because she was all but baring her soul to him and it wasn't getting her anywhere. But Devon knew that she wasn't going to have any peace until she found some way to resolve this.

Her eyes met his. She played her ace card. "I miss you, Cody," she told him.

That look on her face was going to be his undoing, he thought.

"Oh damn, you're making this really hard, Devon."

She raised her eyes to his. "Making *what* hard?" she asked.

He debated saying it, but she left him no choice. So he did.

"Staying away from you," he told her simply.

"Then don't," she entreated.

With his last fiber of resolve, Cody struggled to hold himself in check.

"I don't want you to feel that you're obligated to me in any way." He could see by the look on her face that she didn't understand what he was trying to tell her. He let out a ragged sigh, trying again. "I don't want you thinking that I helped you in order to help myself to you."

And then she understood.

*Idiot*, she thought.

"Did it ever occur to you that maybe, just maybe, I'd *want* you to?" she asked him in a low voice that seemed to undulate throughout his entire being.

He didn't believe that for a second. He couldn't shake the feeling that he'd be taking advantage of her. "Your emotions are all in an uproar and you're confused, Devon," he told her.

"Don't tell me how I feel," she said, raising her voice. "I *know* how I feel and I'm only confused because you did such a U-turn on me. Now, if I did nothing to offend you, why won't you talk to me?" she asked. "Why don't you hang out with Layla and me the way you did before?"

Once he said this, he didn't know how to unsay it. But she left him no choice. There was nothing else that he could do.

"Because I want you," he said simply.

Cody expected her to look upset or at the very least, retreat from him. Quickly. He did not expect her to say, "Thank God."

Cody blinked, certain he hadn't heard her correctly. "What?"

"I said, 'Thank God,'" Devon repeated, her eyes on his.

He'd heard her the first time. That wasn't what he was asking her. "I heard you," he told her. "But—"

The rest of his words died in his throat as Devon

put her arms around his neck, bringing her body up against his.

"Enough talking," she said.

And then, before Cody could say anything further, she pressed her lips against his, initiating a kiss that seemed to go on forever, growing deeper and more passionate with each second that went by.

A moment later, all his good intentions seemed to dissolve. Cody wrapped his arms around her, the feeling of her body against his warming his very soul. Desire suddenly spiked up so high within him that it all but swallowed him whole.

At the very last second, before he felt himself going down for the third and final time, Cody managed to draw his face back from hers, terminating contact even as his body pleaded for him to continue.

"You don't want to do this," he told her.

Devon's soul-melting smile began in her eyes, which crinkled as she informed him, "See, you don't know everything."

"But we can't," he protested. "You just had a baby." He knew nothing about the way a woman's body worked at a time like this, but he was attempting to be cautious for her sake.

"Everything's back in working order. Trust me," she whispered seductively. "I know my own body."

It had been more than six weeks since she'd given birth and prior to that, there had been several months of complete abstinence, not because she hadn't wanted the intimacy, but because Jack didn't. He had come up with one excuse after another to keep her at arm's length. He hadn't so much as kissed her in the last two.

The longing she felt right now was overwhelming.

Cody wanted to resist, to be noble for her sake. But good intentions only went so far and all of his disintegrated in the face of the passion that had come to the surface.

His lips locked with hers, Cody carried Devon over to his bed, gently laying her down as if she was the most precious of packages. A fire had been lit within him, a fire that wasn't going to be easily sated, not until they'd made love.

Maybe not even then.

But again, guilt raised its head and he struggled to put an inch of space between them, giving Devon one last chance to change her mind and come to her senses. He couldn't do any more than that.

"You're sure?" he asked breathlessly.

His question only made her want Cody more. No one had ever cared about her feelings, about how she *felt*, certainly not to this extent.

"I'm sure," she murmured. "If it'll make you feel better, I'll sign an affidavit later," she breathed against his lips. "Now make love to me before I go up in smoke entirely."

She felt his lips curve against hers as he smiled. "Can't have that happening," he told her.

*Finally!*

She kissed him back with a fresh wave of passion that all but submerged them both, a giant tsunami of unleashed desire that only kept building, heightening, making her feel almost frantic as she twisted and turned beneath his large, capable hands.

Cody stroked her—over and over again he stroked

her—bringing her up higher with every pass of his hand, every wild beat of her heart.

It took a huge effort to hold herself in check, to keep from reaching the final climax on her own.

But she wanted more than that, more than just gratification.

She wanted Cody to feel what *she* was feeling. Wanted him to experience what *she* was experiencing. Whatever was going to happen, she wanted it to happen to both of them together because she had no idea what tomorrow might usher in.

She needed this memory to cling to if everything that was transpiring tonight suddenly went away.

Shifting, moving her body along his, Devon reached for him, her fingers deftly caressing his muscular back, slipping along his hard biceps and then, with swift, eager strokes, she brought her hands gliding along his hard thighs. Hearing him moan excited her, bringing her up to an even higher plateau.

She moved ever lower until she managed to come to the very essence of him.

As her hands worked their magic, she could feel Cody responding, could feel his body hardening. Pulsating.

He wanted her and it was time.

Devon parted her legs and arched her back, the invitation unspoken but clear.

Just before his next move, she opened her eyes. She saw that Cody was looking back at her. Their eyes locked even as their bodies forged a union.

His hips moved, thrusting and she mimicked the movement, eager to ride out the wave with him. Eager to feel that final, wild, ecstatic thrill that would have her gasping as it stole her breath away.

She held on to him as hard as she could, absorbing the thrill. Something stirred within her that, until this very second, she hadn't realized had been missing all those other times before, when she'd made love with Jack.

The emotion burst open within her chest like a hungry spring flower searching for the light. It took everything she had not to say the words aloud.

Because she instantly knew what she was feeling, even if she had never felt it before.

Because nothing but love could feel this way.

It took great effort not to shout "I love you" even as the sensation filled her. She knew that she would continue to feel that way long after tonight was just a mere memory.

Happiness mingled with sadness. Because she was in love and because she had no idea what he felt.

*Chapter Sixteen*

Euphoria's hold on him tiptoed away slowly, slipping back into the shadows where it had come from.

Cody held fast for as long as he could. He didn't want to let the moment go, didn't want to allow the outside world and reality to come barging in, taking its place.

All he wanted to do was hold on to this feeling.

Hold on to her.

He lost track of time. Maybe he dozed off, maybe he didn't. But he kept his arm tucked around Devon, comforted by the sound of her even breathing.

Had she fallen asleep, or…?

And then he heard it, heard the tiny cry that swiftly heralded in the outside world like nothing else could.

Devon raised her head from his chest, cocking her ear and listening. He felt her breath rippling along his chest as she sighed.

Devon glanced in his direction. "I'd better get her before she wakes up everyone else."

"Stay," he told her, gently moving her aside so that he could slip out of his bed and look in on Layla. "I'll go see what she wants."

She felt extremely confused by everything that had

transpired tonight, even as her heart quickened just to look at him. But she didn't want him feeling that he needed to help her. The baby was her responsibility.

"But—"

Cody was already shrugging into his jeans. Standing up, he leaned over and kissed the top of her head.

"Just this once, Devon, don't argue," he requested. "I've got this. You get your sleep."

With that, he padded out of the room barefoot and into the baby's new room.

His path was illuminated by the light from the new lamp Devon had gotten at the baby shower. A shy pink lamb was gamboling across the lamp shade. Cody crossed to the crib.

"So what'll it be, Princess?" he asked as he lifted the fussing baby into his arms. Taking a deep whiff of her diaper, he ruled out one reason for the middle-of-the-night summons. "Well, you don't need changing," he concluded. "That leaves hungry or bored."

One look at her small, intent face answered his question for him. "Hungry, it is. What say you and I go downstairs and raid the refrigerator? How does that sound?"

Layla's face was pressed against his chest and he could feel her little lips rooting around.

Tickled, Cody laughed softly. "I guess that answers that."

Holding Layla close to him, Cody made his way down the stairs and into the kitchen. Although for the most part, Devon was still breastfeeding Layla, she had prepared several small bottles of formula to be used just in case.

"What do you say we let Mommy get her beauty rest—not that she needs it," he went on. "You grow up to be half as pretty as your mama, I'm going to have to make sure that all those young bucks out there know that they'll have me to reckon with if they so much as step one inch over the line."

The bottle warmer Devon had received as another gift at the shower was set up on the counter. Cody took out a bottle from the refrigerator and placed it in the warmer. It did its job quickly. He smiled to himself as the timer went off.

"That's a hell—I mean heck—of a lot more efficient than just putting it into a pot of boiling water." Even so, he tested the bottle's contents to make sure it hadn't gotten *too* warm. "Perfect," he murmured. "Okay, let's get you back upstairs."

Cradling Layla against him with one arm, Cody held the bottle with the other and slowly made his way up the stairs back to Layla's room. Cody wasn't accustomed to moving so slowly, but he wasn't about to take a chance on jostling the infant.

When he got to her room, he crossed over to the rocking chair by the window. He sat down.

After positioning the infant, he began to feed her and gently rock at the same time. He hoped the combination of warm milk and rhythmic motion would help Layla fall asleep again.

And after a while, it did.

Despite the hour, Cody sat for a few minutes just looking at her. No doubt about it. Layla held his heart captive in that tiny fist of hers just as much as her mother did.

Ever so slowly, he removed the bottle's nipple from the rosebud lips that had been so intently clamped around it.

He set the bottle aside but continued sitting there for a moment longer, just watching Layla sleep.

FEELING GUILTY, DEVON had gotten out of bed to look in on her daughter and to see if Cody needed help.

What she saw warmed her heart to such an extent she could feel tears gathering in her eyes. If she hadn't already admitted to herself that she was in love with Cody, she would have fallen in love with the man right at this moment.

For however long this lasted, Devon promised herself, she was going to enjoy it and be grateful that their paths, hers and Cody's, had crossed just when she'd needed him. But being with Jack had taught her that nothing lasted forever, so she intended to savor this while she could.

Suppressing a sigh, Devon tiptoed back away from the room.

WHEN HE FINALLY put Layla down and then went back to his own room, Cody found that his bed was empty. Devon had obviously returned to her room.

For a second, he thought of going to her. Not to make love again but just to slip into her bed. He liked the comforting sensation of having her next to him, of holding her. But he had no idea how Devon might react to his presence there. She might think that he wanted to make love again—he did, but that wasn't the main reason he wanted her beside him.

She needed her sleep, he told himself, surrendering the notion. He resigned himself to sleeping alone.

His bed felt cold and empty as he slipped into it.

"ARE YOU UP to meeting someone?" Cody asked Devon suddenly as he walked into the kitchen. He made no effort to hide his excitement. Less than a week had gone by since the parameters of their relationship had shifted.

He'd initially thought about pretending that nothing had happened, but that was a lie. Something *had* happened. And over the course of the next few days, it kept on happening by very mutual consent.

"Who?" she asked as she turned from the stove for a moment.

Whatever she was making smelled really good, he thought absently. As did she, he added as a silent afterthought. Just looking at her stirred him and made him think of things that had nothing to do with cooking.

He paused for a moment to choose his words, but then gave up and just let them come tumbling out. She'd get the gist of this soon enough.

"Her name's Julia Shaw and she's the principal of Forever's only elementary school. She's an old friend," he qualified. "And she'd like to meet you whenever it's convenient."

Devon stopped stirring the beef stew she was making and looked at Cody. She wasn't following him. "Why would she want to meet me, Cody?" she asked. "Just what's this all about?"

"Well, you mentioned that you'd been a substitute teacher in New Mexico and that you were thinking of getting back to teaching someday. I happen to know that one of the teachers at the elementary school is leaving Forever, so I checked it out. I found out that there'll be an opening for a fifth-grade teacher in the fall. Now, I know you said that your goal is to teach at a junior college, but I figure maybe some baby steps might be in order."

Devon was stunned to say the least and very close to speechless as she looked at him. When she finally found her tongue, she had to ask. "How did you manage this?"

The corners of his mouth curved into a grin that could be called nothing short of sexy.

"There are some advantages to living in a small town," he told her. "For one thing, everybody knows everybody—or knows someone who knows the someone you want to meet." Cody realized that he was getting lost in his explanation and so he simplified it. "Bottom line is that Julia would like to meet you and talk to you about your experience."

"Well, I have teaching credentials," she said. "But I actually didn't teach for that long."

"Then that shouldn't be a problem," Cody concluded. He knew for a fact that Julia was actively searching for a teacher to plug up the unexpected hole in her staff. And then it occurred to him that Devon looked less than excited about this prospect. Had he misunderstood something? "I mean, if you still want to be a teacher."

"Oh, I do," she assured him quickly. And then she sighed. Nothing was black-and-white anymore. "But things have gotten a little complicated the last few weeks. I mean, I'd need to find someone to watch Layla for me while I was teaching every day, so—"

"We'll come up with something," he promised her. "That's not a problem." He handed her a folded piece of paper. On it was Julia's private number. "Why don't you talk to Julia and make an appointment to meet with her?" he suggested.

Devon opened the paper and stared at it for a moment. "Really?" she asked, unable to believe that it was going to be this easy. Almost *too* easy, she couldn't help thinking.

He smiled as he went to pick up Layla out of her portable playpen.

"Really," he assured her before he looked at the infant and cooed, "Hi, Princess. Miss me?"

Devon pressed her lips together as she watched Cody with her daughter. *Temporary, it's just temporary*, she reminded herself. *Don't get used to it.*

But it was hard not to.

ALL TWELVE GRADES of Forever's school system could essentially be found within the confines of one building. The first eight grades were located in the larger wing of the building while the last four were in the other, far smaller wing.

In the center, connecting the two wings, was not just the lone kindergarten class but a preschool class, as well. There were only three children enrolled for the fall term in the preschool class. The teacher who oversaw the kindergarten class did double duty with preschoolers as well since each class was held at a different time of the day.

Accustomed to larger schools, not to mention

larger classes, Devon thought the whole thing seemed charming and quaint. Julia Shaw had arranged to meet with her on the school grounds and had taken her on a tour of the entire building before conducting the interview.

Cody had insisted on taking the day off to bring her to the school and to introduce her to Julia.

"You don't have to do this, you know," Devon had protested when he'd told her. "I can drive over myself," she reminded him, since she had her own vehicle.

He'd let her talk until she was finished and then said, "Humor me."

"Thank you," she murmured as an afterthought.

He'd merely smiled at her and replied, "Don't mention it."

He made her feel special and beautiful for no reason at all, but she kept waiting for the other shoe to drop—because it always did.

THE INTERVIEW, CONDUCTED in the principal's office, lasted all of thirty minutes and that included the tour. Julia Shaw was an attractive blonde who looked more like a model than a newly appointed school principal.

When the interview ended, Julia sat back in her chair and smiled at her as she nodded. "Well, I'm satisfied," she told Devon. And then she extended her hand. "Welcome aboard, Devon. The fifth-grade position is all yours."

Devon looked at her in disbelief. "Don't you want to send for my records first to verify everything?" she asked uncertainly.

"Yes, I will definitely check your credentials and references, but I'm confident in my decision."

"Are you sure?"

"Why?" Julia asked her, amused. "Did you lie about them?"

That caught Devon completely off guard. It took her a second to find her tongue. "No, of course not."

Julia spread her hands. "Well, then I know all I need to know. Besides, I went to school with Cody. If he's vouching for you, that's certainly good enough for me," she informed the younger woman. "Moreover, you sound as if you really like children."

"Oh, I do," Devon assured the principal with feeling. She loved not just their innocence but their honesty, as well. As far as she was concerned, children were far more trustworthy than adults.

"I thought so," Julia said with approval. "Well, here's the employment packet the board makes me hand out. Just fill out the forms and bring all that back with you on the first day of school. I'm planning on holding a meeting before then, but I'll let you know the date once it's set." Rising to her feet, she coaxed, "C'mon, I'll walk you out."

Julia led the way through the hall. Stopping at the front door, Julia pushed it opened and held it for Forever's newest teacher.

Cody was waiting just outside the entrance. As soon as the door opened, he crossed to it.

"How'd she do, Jules?" Cody asked the woman beside Devon.

"Thanks to you, a crisis has been avoided. We have our teacher," Julia told him. Looking at Devon, the woman smiled. "See you in the fall."

Once the principal had retreated back into the building, Cody beamed at Devon. "Congratulations! Why don't we go to Miss Joan's and I'll buy you lunch so we can celebrate?"

Her smile was somewhat forced. "No, that's all right."

"You're not hungry?" he asked. For someone who had just gotten the job he thought she was hoping for, Devon didn't exactly strike him as being overjoyed— or even very happy.

"I'm too excited to eat," she told him. "Everything's happening so fast."

Cody abruptly stopped walking and just looked at her. "What?" she asked.

"Nothing," he replied. "I'm just waiting to see your nose grow."

She blinked. "Excuse me?"

"Like Pinocchio when he told a lie," he explained.

Indignant, she squared her shoulders. "I'm not lying," she protested. And then she sighed. Cody was going to keep looking at her until she came clean. "You didn't tell me you knew her that well."

"Knew who that well?" he asked. Devon had managed to lose him without taking a single step.

"The principal. Ms. Shaw. Julia," she finally said.

He shrugged. "I went to school with her," he admitted, and then asked, "So?"

She shrugged, embarrassed by how she was feeling, but unable to shake it off. "Nothing. She just seemed rather taken with you, that's all. Did you two date or anything?"

"No to both questions,' he told her. And then it hit him. "You're not jealous of Julia, are you?"

"Of course not," she said much too quickly.

"Because there's nothing to be jealous of," he assured her. "She had a crush on Connor for a while, but I doubt if she even noticed me until I asked her about a teaching position for you."

"How could she not notice you?" Devon challenged. The woman had to be blind not to react to Cody's looks, Devon thought.

"Very, very easily," he assured her. "And I think it's very cute that you're jealous."

"I am *not* jealous," she retorted, and then thought better of it. There was really no point in protesting the obvious. "Well, maybe a little."

He laughed and then he kissed her, right there in the street. Her heart shot up to her throat and then fell down again, pounding hard. "You're messing with my head," she told him.

"Seems only fair because you're messing with mine," he told her as he held the passenger door open for her.

"I need a clear head to think about my next move," she said as she got in.

He rounded the hood and got in on the driver's side. "Which is?" he asked.

"Finding a place for Layla and me," she told him. The words tasted almost bitter in her mouth. "I mean, that's the next logical step, isn't it? I can't expect to impose on you and your family indefinitely."

He studied her face before answering. "I wasn't aware that you were imposing," he told her. "But if you feel awkward about staying now that we've—" How could he put this delicately, he wondered, searching for the words. He finally settled on a euphemism.

"—now that we've *been* together, I understand. Although," he went on as he put his key into the ignition, "if it'll make you feel better, what happened the other night—and the nights after that—doesn't have to happen again."

Devon felt her stomach sinking. "Then you *do* think it was a mistake," she concluded.

"If it makes you leave, then yes," he told her simply. Then he felt honor bound to add, "But honestly, no, I don't think it was a mistake." He challenged, "How could I?"

Devon shook her head. She didn't know what to think. "You're confusing me."

He put the question to her point-blank. "Do you want to move?"

Devon bit her bottom lip, and then said, "I should."

"That's not what I asked you," he pointed out. "I said do you *want* to move."

This time Devon pressed her lips together, knowing what she thought she should say and what she actually *wanted* to say.

"I've never been part of a household where people care about each other, where they watch out for each other. I have no right to be here, but I do know that I am very grateful for the time I got to spend at your ranch with your family."

"It doesn't have to end," he told her. "At the very least, there's no rush for you to leave anytime soon. Listen, we're all crazy about Layla and, this way, there's always someone there for her, freeing you up to do what you need to."

"But that's imposing," Devon insisted.

There was that word again. Cody was not about to back off. "We don't see it that way."

"You can't speak for the others," she told him. For all he knew, his siblings were counting the minutes until she left.

"Sure I can. After you've been through as much as we have together, you get to know what the others are thinking and feeling. And I can tell you with certainty that if I let you move out without at least *trying* to talk you out of it, the others will have my head, no doubt about it. I might not be the best-looking guy around, but I promise I'll look even worse without a head."

She had no idea why, but that struck her as funny. So funny that she couldn't stop laughing for a couple of minutes.

Finally, when she did, she told him, "You're crazy, you know that?"

*Yeah, crazy about you*, Cody thought.

"Whatever you say," he said out loud. "Now, about that lunch at Miss Joan's," he reminded Devon. "This way, you can tell her the good news. Miss Joan loves being the first one to hear good news."

Devon inclined her head. He'd won her over with that argument. "Okay, sounds good."

"Knew I'd convince you," he said.

Now all he had to do was convince her about the rest, Cody added silently. And that, he had a feeling, was not going to be easy.

## Chapter Seventeen

Despite her background, Devon had never been one who allowed herself to be consumed by worry. For the most part, she'd always managed to face life with a healthy resilience, determined not just to take whatever fate threw her way but to triumph over it. No matter how bad the situation might be, she had always found a way to stay true to herself and forge on. She felt that, as long as she kept moving, she would survive.

But all that was when she only had herself to think about. She didn't have just herself to think about anymore. Now she had to view things through the eyes of a mother, always mindful that there was a little person who was totally dependent on her. A little person whom she needed to watch over and take care of.

Not exactly an easy feat when she didn't even have a dollar to her name.

That was what Jack had left her when he took off—nothing. He'd stolen not just her love but everything he could put his hands on. That included her credit cards and the money in her wallet. All the money she had managed to save up.

All the money she had in the whole world.

Devon had been quick to cancel all of her credit cards—there'd been only two—but the money, perforce, was a lost cause. As was ever getting back the necklace and earrings her mother had left her.

Being completely penniless made her extremely aware of the fact that she couldn't provide even the most basic of things for her baby.

Thanks to Cody, she had a job that would begin in the fall, but that still didn't pay any of the bills right now. The fact that she couldn't pay for anything had her frustrated beyond words, not to mention exceedingly hemmed in.

Stress and tension all but radiated from her.

Certainly this tension was not lost on Cody. He felt it the moment he got home and walked into the kitchen to see her.

"Something wrong?" he asked.

It was far better to meet any problem head-on than to pretend that it wasn't there. In Cody's opinion, the latter approach only made things fester and grow worse. Besides, he preferred things out in the open.

Devon hardly spared him a look. With Layla dozing in her bassinet in the corner, Devon was busy preparing dinner.

"No," she bit off.

Cody didn't believe her. "You're pacing," he pointed out.

She shrugged off his observation. "I'm getting dinner ready."

Cody frowned slightly. It was time to correct that, he thought. "About that—" he began.

Devon stopped dead, but she still didn't turn toward him. "Getting sick of my cooking?" she guessed, her voice on edge.

He'd always been good at picking up both blatant signals and subtle nuances. There was a definite shift in her voice as well as her personality. Devon was being defensive for no reason that he could see.

"No, nobody's even remotely tired of your cooking, but we talked it over and decided that it wasn't fair to keep having you make the meals, no matter how good they are." Cassidy had even voiced the feeling that it was taking advantage of Devon.

Devon raised her chin as if she was preparing for a fight.

"You talked it over?" she repeated. "When?"

Definitely defensive, Cody thought. He was going to have to tread lightly here until he discovered exactly what this was all about.

"Last night," he answered mildly. "There's no doubt about the fact that you really have a gift when it comes to cooking," he assured her. "But we feel that we've been taking unfair advantage of you by *letting* you do all of it these last two months."

That was how she was paying them back for allowing her to live there. She thought they'd already had this discussion. "What else am I supposed to do?" she asked, some of her annoyance coming through.

Cody shrugged. He hadn't thought of anything specific. "Something else," he told her. "You have a life."

"Not really," she countered almost defiantly.

"Okay," he said, taking her by the hand and leading her off to the side. They were alone in the kitchen, but bringing her into the alcove created more privacy in case someone else walked in on them. "What is this *really* all about?" he asked.

She lifted her chin again. "I don't know what you're talking about." She sniffed.

Cody continued watching her, determined to wait her out. When she said nothing, he resorted to coaxing. "Level with me, Devon. What's bothering you?"

She wanted to snap and tell him to stop badgering her, that there was nothing wrong, nothing bothering her. But even as the words rose to her lips, she owed him the truth. There *was* something bothering her.

"Layla needs to go in for her two-month checkup," she told him.

"Okay," Cody allowed, waiting for Devon to get to what was bothering her.

Devon threw up her hands impatiently. "I can't take her."

Cody asked the first thing that came to his mind. "Something wrong with your truck?"

Devon closed her eyes, searching for a vein of inner strength. "No—"

"Because if there is," Cody continued, "I can take the two of you in. No problem."

"It's not the truck," she firmly emphasized. Devon found she had to struggle not to raise her voice.

"Then what is it?" Cody asked patiently.

So far, Devon seemed to be talking in riddles and he really hoped that they were coming closer to the problem so he could know what was bothering her and what omissions he was dealing with.

Devon threw up her hands again. "I can't afford it," she cried. "I don't have any money to pay the doctor." Just admitting it embarrassed her.

"Is that all?" he asked, relieved that it wasn't anything that was actually serious.

"That's not an 'all,'" Devon declared, frustrated. "That's *everything*."

Didn't he see that? Didn't he see how awful it felt not to be able to provide for her daughter's basic needs *at all*?

Cody had a solution, but he tested the waters slowly, not know how it might affect Devon. "I can pay for it," he volunteered.

Her eyes almost blazed as she cried "No!"

The woman just had too much pride as far as he was concerned. It made things difficult.

"All right," he qualified. "I can *lend* you the money to pay for it."

Devon shook her head. "I already owe you too much."

"There's no running tally on any of this," he told her.

Her pride was wounded and hemorrhaging. "I told you before, I am *not* a charity case."

That again, Cody thought. It took effort to curb his impatience. "And no one said you were," he insisted. "Look, did it ever occur to you that it might make me *feel good* to help you?"

"Why would it?" she asked. "You've got better things to do with your money than throw it away like that," she insisted.

"My money, my decision. Besides," Cody continued, raising his voice to stop her from saying anything further, "we do things differently here. A lot of the people the docs treat at the clinic either pay the visits off slowly or make a trade."

"Trade?" Devon repeated. She wasn't sure what he meant by that.

Cody smiled. "One hand washes the other. Like you cooking for us in exchange for your room and board," he pointed out, hoping that would put a lid on the subject once and for all.

But Devon shook her head. "It just doesn't feel right."

They could go around and around about this all night. "It's right if we say it's right," he told her once and for all.

Rather than concede, Devon took the so-called argument they were having in a completely different direction.

"I'm getting much too dependent on you," Devon complained quietly.

He kind of liked having her depend on him. It made him feel useful in an entirely different light. "And that's a bad thing because…?"

Devon stared at him. "Because someday, when I least expect it, you'll grow tired of carrying me and suddenly, the rug'll be pulled out from under my feet and I'll go plummeting down into this deep, dark abyss."

Okay, now it was making sense to him. "That's a very colorful scenario, but it's not going to happen."

"There are no guarantees in life," she insisted.

Cody's eyes met hers. He felt the same ache within him that he always did lately. An ache that had its roots in fear. Fear that she was going to just disappear on him. That one day, he'd reach out for her and she wouldn't be there.

Wouldn't be anywhere.

"Sometimes, there are," he told her quietly.

"Like what?" she challenged.

He spelled it out for her. "Like I can guarantee that I'm going to feel the same way about you tomorrow that I do now and that I will the day after that and the day after that—to the nth degree," he said.

"What way?" she asked, feeling shaky inside. She was cornering him and she knew it. But she already knew that Cody wasn't the kind of man who lied and, if she pressed him for an answer, he would give her an honest one. She was counting on it and hoping against hope that it would be enough to break through her wall of fear and convince her.

"I love you," he told her quietly. "I'm not Jack," he insisted. "Get that through your head. I'm not going anywhere. Ever."

*I love you.*

She stared at him. She'd heard the words before. Heard them and clung to them and they had turned out to be as binding as soap bubbles. Jack had told her he loved her and then took off soon after that without a backward glance.

"You don't mean that," she said flatly.

Cody measured his words carefully. "No disrespect, Devon, but you don't have any right to tell me what I mean or don't mean. If I say I love you, then that's what I mean." A little more fiercely, he repeated, "I love you."

"Why?" she asked. "*Why* do you love me?"

Rather than get annoyed with her for pressing him, he did his best to make her understand. "For more reasons than you can possibly imagine. Looking back, I probably fell in love with you the first moment I laid eyes on you."

As she recalled it, she had her legs spread out and she was screaming, not to mention that she'd looked like a mess. "Not my finest moment."

"Oh, but it was," he said. And then he grinned. "And I want to love you through every moment for the rest of my life."

She shook her head, unable to accept that. "You just feel sorry for me."

"No," he corrected, "I feel sorry for *me* because you're giving me such a hard time over this." He took hold of her shoulders to keep her in place and to force her to look at him as he spoke. "Now, you may not like hearing it and I really can't help that, but I love you." He took a breath and went for broke. "And I'd like to marry you."

Stunned, her mouth dropped open. "No," she whispered in disbelief.

Cody took it as a rejection, but he tried not to let it slice him up inside.

"Not the answer I wanted to hear, but there's no hurry. You can take your time, think it over, work it out." He emphasized, "Like I said, there's no hurry. Because I'll still be here when you finally realize that maybe marrying me isn't such a bad thing. Bottom line is *I am not going anywhere.*"

She realized that she'd stopped breathing and took in a deep one now before asking, "You're serious?"

Out of the corner of his eye, he saw Cole about to enter the kitchen and he waved his brother back. Cole took the hint and disappeared.

Facing Devon, Cody's expression was the soul of

solemnity. "I've never been more serious in my entire life."

Devon never took her eyes off him. "You're not just saying this to make me feel better?" Devon asked.

"No," Cody corrected. "I'm saying this to make *me* feel better."

As if she believed that. "Why would you want to marry me?" she challenged, silently demanding that he somehow convince her.

Maybe he needed to enumerate the reasons for her, at least to some extent. He began with the most obvious. "Because you're beautiful. I look at you and my heart all but stops. Because you're a good person. You could have taken advantage of all of us—we would have gladly let you—but you didn't. And maybe most of all because I need you to need me."

The reasons were all valid, but somehow, she just couldn't see how they applied to her. She didn't feel worthy of that sort of sentiment or capable of generating it in someone else.

"Is that all?" she asked quietly.

"No, that's just the beginning," Cody answered. "But I promise that if and when you do decide to marry me, I'll make sure that you never live to regret it, not even for a single moment."

"That's a tall order," Devon told him, struggling really hard not to smile.

"In case you haven't noticed, I live up to all my promises," he told her with a touch of pride. "Just ask around."

She didn't have to. She knew the kind of man he was. He was offering her the world on a platter. It didn't seem fair to him. "I don't have anything to give you," she told him.

"Now, there you're wrong," Cody contradicted. "You have yourself to give and I couldn't ask for a more precious gift," he told her honestly. "And don't worry," he quickly told her, "I'm not going to ask you for an answer yet. I told you you could take your time and you can. Take as long as you want—as long as, eventually, you come up with the right answer, the one I need to hear." He added, "No pressure."

"Yes," Devon said.

"Yes, we have an understanding?" he asked, not quite sure what she was telling him.

"Yes," Devon repeated. Her eyes had locked with his and remained that way.

"Yes to the understanding?" he asked again uncertainly. She still wasn't making herself clear and he refused to jump the gun in case he was wrong. Because being wrong would hurt too much.

"Yes to the question," she told him.

"Which question?" he asked.

The corners of her mouth began to curve. "The only question that counts."

He looked at her apprehensively, still afraid that he was grasping at the one thing he wanted to hear. But he knew that he couldn't just walk away from this without knowing, without being *positive*.

"This question—Devon, will you marry me?" he asked.

Her eyes crinkled as she threw her arms around his neck and brought her mouth up to his.

"Yes," she repeated with feeling and then, in case they were still bogged down in rhetoric, she made herself perfectly clear by saying, "Yes, Cody, I will marry you."

His heart all but leaped out of his chest as he asked for one final confirmation. "You're sure?"

Her eyes were laughing as she said, "I'm sure."

"I'm not pressuring you?" he asked her.

"No, you're not pressuring me." Her eyes were smiling now. "You are, however, driving me crazy."

"Well, that's only fair," he told her as his arms around her tightened. "Because you're doing the same to me."

She didn't want to talk. More than anything, she needed him to kiss her, to finally seal this bargain they had struck up. "Shut up and kiss me."

He pulled her even closer as he brought his mouth within a hair's breadth of hers. "Oh, with more pleasure than you can possibly imagine."

"Does this mean someone else is making dinner?" she asked teasingly.

There was mischief in his eyes as he asked, "What do you think?"

"I don't want to think," she told him. "I just want to feel."

"That can be arranged," he promised her.

"Show me," she whispered.

He did.

And Layla slept through it all.

Both her mother and her father-to-be took that as a good omen.

# Epilogue

Devon looked at her reflection in the full-length mirror in the church's antechamber. She hardly recognized the person in the wedding gown looking back at her. That person was positively glowing.

She put her hand over her stomach, willing the butterflies away.

They stayed put.

"Maybe we should have eloped," she said, addressing the other reflection she saw in the mirror.

Cassidy, resplendent in a blue maid-of-honor dress, was fussing with the bottom of Devon's wedding dress, making certain that the veil's train wasn't trapped beneath it.

"Don't you even dare think about it," Cassidy warned. "This is the first McCullough wedding and there's a church full of people out there, not to mention your little fifth-graders, who would be heartbroken if you suddenly turned tail and became Forever's version of the runaway bride," she admonished.

"Runaway brides leave grooms at the altar," Devon pointed out. "I don't want to leave Cody at the altar. I just don't want everyone watching me show up to marry him."

"Too late," Cassidy said. She dropped the train and stood back for a moment to admire her handiwork. "You're good to go," she pronounced happily.

Cassidy glanced over to the corner where Layla was sitting up in a colorfully decorated car seat. She was wearing an infant's version of Cassidy's dress. "Too bad she's too little to be your flower girl, but I guess you can't have everything."

"You're wrong, there," Devon corrected her. "I *do* have everything." She smiled at Cassidy. "I'm even getting the sister I always wanted."

Cassidy laughed. "Just try getting rid of me." There was a knock on the door and Cassidy exchanged glances with the bride. "I didn't think that Connor was coming for you for another ten minutes." Because her father had long since passed away, Devon had asked Connor to give her away. "He's probably early to make sure you're not changing your mind."

Devon shook her head. "Not a chance."

Cassidy opened the door. Then she tried to close it again.

"You're not supposed to see the bride before the wedding, Cody," she admonished. "Don't you know anything? It's supposed to be bad luck."

Cody stuck his foot in to block his sister from shutting the door. "I just want to give her something," he told Cassidy. "I thought she would want to wear it during the ceremony."

"Let him in, Cassidy," Devon said.

"It's against tradition," Cassidy insisted.

"So's everything that's happened in my life so far," Devon told her.

She felt that if Cody wanted to see her right before

the ceremony, it had to be about something important. Telling him he couldn't because of some ancient superstition wouldn't be starting out their marriage on the right foot.

Cassidy frowned. "Okay, but this is against my better judgment," she said just before she opened the door farther. "Okay, buster, what's so important it can't wait?" she demanded of her brother.

"I'd like a minute alone with my fiancée if you don't mind," Cody said, amused that his sister had turned into a guard dog in a bridesmaid dress.

Cassidy picked up Layla. "Let's get you situated out there, Princess." Since Cassidy and her brothers were all in the wedding party, Miss Joan had volunteered to hold the baby for the duration of the ceremony. "Make it quick," she told Cody. "Connor's due in less than ten minutes."

"This won't take long," Cody said. As Cassidy left, he turned to face Devon and really looked at her. She took his breath away. "I didn't think you could be any more beautiful than you already were, but I was wrong."

"Is that what you came to say?" Devon asked. She was no longer afraid that he was going to call the wedding off at the last minute, but, for the life of her, she couldn't come up with a reason for Cody showing up like this just before the ceremony.

"No," he replied. "I came to give you this. I thought you might want it."

"This" was what he was holding in his hand. He held it up in front of her before he drew back his fingers. There in the palm of his hand was a necklace and a pair of earrings.

*Her* necklace and earrings. She would have known them anywhere.

Her eyes widened as she stared first at the items and then at him. "Where did you get these?"

"Then they are yours?" He was fairly certain that they were, but he wanted her to confirm it.

"Yes!" she cried, taking both from him and looking at them in wonder. She never thought she'd see the necklace and earrings again. "Where—? How—?"

"They were in a pawnshop thirty miles outside of Houston." It had taken him all this time to locate the items, circulating Jack's photo to all the pawnshops between Forever and Houston. Jack was nowhere to be found, but at least the jewelry was. He felt extremely triumphant about locating it, especially when he saw the look in Devon's eyes. It was priceless. "I thought you might want to wear them."

There were tears in her eyes as she put the earrings on. Then, turning her back to Cody, she gave him the necklace so that he could fasten the gold clasp for her. She held very still, almost afraid to breathe. She was that happy.

"I don't know how to thank you!"

Finished, Cody turned her slowly around to face him. "Don't worry, we have the rest of our lives together to work on that."

The wedding march was starting. In the next moment, Connor was in the doorway. He rapped once.

"Time," he declared, giving his younger brother a piercing look.

Cody grinned, withdrawing. "It sure is," he agreed. "See you at the altar," he told Devon just before he hurried away.

Connor shook his head as he offered Devon his arm. "Well, at least you know what you're getting into," he said to her.

Devon could only beam as she replied, love in every word, "I certainly do."

* * * * *

# MILLS & BOON®

## *Cherish*™

**EXPERIENCE THE ULTIMATE RUSH OF FALLING IN LOVE**

## sneak peek at next month's titles...

**In stores from 20th October 2016:**

**Christmas Baby for the Princess** – Barbara Wallace *and*
**The Maverick's Holiday Surprise** – Karen Rose Smith
**Greek Tycoon's Mistletoe Proposal** – Kandy Shepherd
*and* **A Child Under His Tree** – Allison Leigh

**In stores from 3rd November 2016:**

**The Billionaire's Prize** – Rebecca Winters *and*
**The Rancher's Expectant Christmas** – Karen Templeton
**The Earl's Snow-Kissed Proposal** – Nina Milne *and*
**Callie's Christmas Wish** – Merline Lovelace

*Just can't wait?*
Buy our books online a month before they hit the shops!
**www.millsandboon.co.uk**

**Also available as eBooks.**

# MILLS & BOON®

## EXCLUSIVE EXCERPT

When Dea Caracciolo agrees to attend a sporting event as tycoon Guido Rossano's date, sparks fly!

*Read on for a sneak preview of*
**THE BILLIONAIRE'S PRIZE**
*the final instalment of Rebecca Winters'*
*thrilling Cherish trilogy*
**THE MONTINARI MARRIAGES**

The dark blue short-sleeved dress with small red poppies Dea was wearing hugged her figure, then flared from the waist to the knee. With every step the material danced around her beautiful legs, imitating the flounce of her hair she wore down the way he liked it. Talk about his heart failing him!

"Dea—"

Her searching gaze fused with his. "I hope it's all right." The slight tremor in her voice betrayed her fear that she wasn't welcome. If she only knew...

"You've had an open invitation since we met." Nodding his thanks to Mario, he put his arm around her shoulders and drew her inside the suite.

He slid his hands in her hair. "You're the most beautiful sight this man has ever seen." With uncontrolled hunger he lowered his mouth to hers and began to devour her. Over the announcer's voice and the roar of the crowd, he heard her little moans of pleasure as their bodies merged and they drank deeply.

When she swayed in his arms, he half carried her over to the couch where they could give in to their frenzied needs. She smelled heavenly. One kiss grew into another until she became his entire world. He'd never known a feeling like this and lost track of time and place.

"Do you know what you do to me?" he whispered against her lips with feverish intensity.

"I came for the same reason."

Her admission pulled him all the way under. Once in a while the roar of the crowd filled the room, but that didn't stop him from twining his legs with hers. He desired a closeness they couldn't achieve as long as their clothes separated them.

"I want you, *bellissima*. I want you all night long. Do you understand what I'm saying?"

# MILLS & BOON®

## Why shop at millsandboon.co.uk?

Each year, thousands of romance readers find their perfect read at millsandboon.co.uk. That's because we're passionate about bringing you the very best romantic fiction. Here are some of the advantages of shopping at www.millsandboon.co.uk:

* **Get new books first**—you'll be able to buy your favourite books one month before they hit the shops

* **Get exclusive discounts**—you'll also be able to buy our specially created monthly collections, with up to 50% off the RRP

* **Find your favourite authors**—latest news, interviews  and new releases for all your favourite authors and series on our website, plus ideas for what to try next

* **Join in**—once you've bought your favourite books, don't forget to register with us to rate, review and join in the discussions

Visit **www.millsandboon.co.uk**
for all this and more today!